b...
in the
rewarding
from the gut
around it all, is
Britain's neglected
comparison with the w.
Kelman. That's how good, a   ...dlessly
fascinating this collection is.

Soulful fiction that comes from the heart, written with
imagination and style. Russ Litten is a special talent.

Russ Litten is one of Yorkshire's finest contemporary
writers. His voice is loaded with slarter and salt, yet full
of compassion and pathos. We do not pity his
characters, but feel a sense of empathy towards them,
their hard scratch existence is brought to life on the
page. This collection reveals the underbelly of Hull, the
flipside of City of Culture. It is an essential read for all
who are curious about this wild, complex and vibrant
city.

You resent these stories because they remind you of it all. The fruitlessness of regular working life, its conditions, its traps. And the existence immediately below that. Despair. These are the final two tiers before the void.

Jason Williamson
Sleaford Mods

We Know What We Are

Russ Litten

We Know What We Are
Copyright © 2018 Russ Litten

The right of Russ Litten to be identified as the author of this work
has been asserted by him in accordance with the Copyright, Designs
and Patents Act 1988.

This book is a work of fiction. Any resemblance between these
fictional characters and actual persons, living or dead, is purely
coincidental.

Published by Obliterati Press
2018

ISBN: 978-1-9997528-2-8

www.obliteratipress.com

Russ Litten is the author of the novels *Scream If You Want To Go Faster*, *Swear Down* and *Kingdom*. He has also written for film, TV and radio and is one half of the electronic story-telling outfit Cobby & Litten (*My People Come From The Sea*, *Boothferry*). Russ lives and works in Kingston Upon Hull.

ACKNOWLEDGEMENTS

Some of these stories first appeared in
other publications: Mendicant Bookworks
(USA), Pearl Magazine (USA), Verbal (UK)
and Decent Spread (UK).

Thanks are extended to Steve Cobby,
Martin Lewsley, Michael Gratzke and the
people of KUH.

This book is dedicated to the memory of
Ronald Herbert Litten

Contents

Blade

I watched them put that blade in. Woke me up they did, that big crane and lorry and all them vans clattering about. I heard 'em all come beep-beep-beeping into the square. About half three in the morning, this was. I wrapped me sleeping bag tight round meself and peeped out from behind the wall. Whirling blue lights and coppers and blokes stood about in orange vests, yapping into radios. None of 'em noticed me; they were all too enthralled with this massive big blade thing being hoisted about.

I was proper freaked out at first. I'd just woke up. And I mean, what the actual fuck was it? What was it for? This was summat straight out the blue for me. I'd not heard nowt about this. I guessed it was all to do with that City of Culture, though. Like them films on the buildings. I liked them; they were brilliant they was, mind-blowing really. Especially that bit when City Hall set on fire. All the sirens and flames and bricks exploding. That was proper ace, that was.

This blade thing though... well, I dint know it was supposed to be a blade until someone later on that day told me that's what it was. It looked more like a giant bone, I thought. Like if they'd digged up a dinosaur. The leg off a big T-Rex. It was mad, right, coz I'd even been dreaming about dinosaurs a couple of nights before. Dreamt I lived in a cave and I was tucked up all warm and safe except there was all these monsters roaring and stamping about outside. That's what happens when yer stop smoking and drinking and what have yer; yer start dreaming. I liked having proper dreams again though, even the frightening ones.

I tried waking Johnner up so he could watch an'all, but he was proper sparked. I wanted him to see it so I'd know I wasn't dreaming. I couldn't quite believe it. It was mad, all that light and noise in the middle of the night. Like a spaceship had landed. I stood and watched them trying to swing it into place. They had a right job gerrin it all sorted out. At one bit it was just propped upwards, like a giant finger pointing up to heaven. It stayed like that for ages. I couldn't work out what they were trying to do. After a bit I was nithered, so I got curled up beneath the blast heater again, under the blankets next to Johnner snoring his lugs off.

But when I woke up later he was gone. This was about half five, six. Dark, still; just the edge of the sun peeping up over the buildings. All the lorries and vans and the crane and the blokes in orange were still there. And they still hadn't got that blade in.

I dint know what to think at first, coz Johnner had never gone off before. I mean, we'd had rows and that, obviously, and he'd storm off in the street and that, but he'd never before got off without saying where he was going. We had a vow to stay together and he just wouldn't do that, mate. Never in a million years would he break that sacred vow, coz Johnner is the truest, most beautiful person I have ever known. He can be useless as well like, but he can't help that. People can't help how they are, can they? But there's not an ounce of nastiness in him.

Anyhow, I want too worried at first. I knew he wouldn't have gone far, coz truth is he can't cope without me. Thinking about it now though, I should have sussed that summat was up. He'd been dead quiet all the day before. It want his depression or just him being quiet – it was summat else. Yer get to sense it when yer've been with a person a while. Yer get to recognise the signs. I was worried at first that he ant took his meds, but he'd gone and got his prescription the day before. Two months' worth, so it want that.

When I first got with Johnner he was all over the shop. Vulnerable. Took everything to heart, he did. Slightest thing would crush him. I got him sorted down at Dock Street and helped him with all his forms and that. We just clicked straight away. Joined at the hip from that day on, we was. Even when they kicked us out – for fuck all, really, just a few cans – even then, we stuck tight together and made the vow, till death do us part. Stronger together, that's what we said. So that's what we did. We got through everything together, good times and bad. Even when we got that tent and pitched it up in a graveyard and them bastard kids set it on fire on day four, he still dint let his head drop and he dint go back to using, and do yer know why? Coz I'd trained him. By then, I'd proper trained him. I told him, yer've got to be hard, mate, no matter what fate throws at yer. Yer can't just lay down and die or start feeling sorry for yerself, not even for one tiny split second, coz that's what the bastards want. They feed off misery, they do. They love it, mate; absolutely love it. Yer show one hint of weakness and they all come piling in.

So even though he'd never gone off before I want that concerned. Not at first. Yeah, he's just got a bee in his bonnet about summat, I thought. Some daft bit of trivia. He got like that sometimes. A worrier, was Johnner. He'll be back, I thought.

I went and had a wash in the bogs on the pier then headed back to our usual spot near Prinny Quay. I dint do too bad that morning; I got about two pound forty and a cup of tea off that nice woman who always passes on her way to work; her with the white coat and big headphones. She always says hello and good morning or afternoon, even if she dunt give me owt. Sometimes, that's nearly as good as money, someone just smiling and saying hiya. That morning, she got me a cup of tea and I sat and made it last till it went nearly cold and I watched them mess about with that blade. There were telly cameras and people with microphones an'all by this point. Everyone stood about gawping. I sat and watched it all, keeping one eye out for Johnner, expecting to see him come limping across the square, his sleeping bag slung over his shoulder.

But it got to near dinner-time and he still ant come. I was starting to get a bit worried by this point, but I thought, no, stay here, stay put; he's bound to turn up sooner or later.

They eventually got the blade set down proper how they wanted it. It stretched right over the road and all the traffic passed underneath. The tops of the buses were just missing it. They must have measured it all out exactly. The very tip of it was nearly touching the top of Punch. It looked proper mad. There was a group of them volunteers in blue jackets handing out leaflets near the thickest end. People were walking underneath it and reaching up, tapping the bottom of the thing. I went and had a look. I couldn't believe how big it was when you got up close and stood underneath it. And it felt real smooth when you touched it. I thought it would be all cold, like, I dunno, a statue or summat, but it felt warm. I asked one of the bluecoats what it was made out of and she said resin. I wish it was, I said, I'd break a big lump off and go and sit in the cemetery. I was joking, coz I don't smoke or drink or do owt no more. She just looked at me, though. She told me it was part of a wind turbine from Siemens. This lad wandered up and started banging on about how that effing thing could have paid to sleep fifty homeless every night for a year, but the bluecoat told him it had been donated for free. Worth a lot of money, though, she said. How much, I asked her. She dint know, but she said it was loads; thousands. We stood and looked up at it, stretching away over our heads.

Anyway, after a bit I started getting proper anxious coz there was still no sign of Johnner. He had his meds on him, so I want really worried about that, but what if he forgot to take 'em? What I was most worried about was if he bumped into Skinner and all them lot and they'd have a drink on 'em.

It want a girlfriend-boyfriend thing at first with me and Johnner. I told him, I made it clear: I don't do blokes. I told him I was a lesbian, which want true, but that's what I used to say. I dint know what I was, to be truthful. All I knew was that I fucking hated men – all of 'em – and if any of the bastards came near me they got a mouthful, and if that dint see 'em off, a kick in the bollocks or me nails in their face. But Johnner want like that. He's gentle, is Johnner. He has the soul of a beautiful gentleman. He's like someone you'd imagine in the olden days of Queen

Victoria, like a dead gracious gentleman who'd take his hat off when he greeted you or lay his coat across a puddle. Dint hardly even swear when I first met him. He was proper sweet and kind-hearted, was Johnner.

I remember asking him for his story, how he ended up out here, and he'd basically let these blokes do a grow in his flat coz he was skint and needed the money. He got busted and refused to grass, so he ended up doing six month. Came out, flat gone, bird deserted him, all his benefits cut. So that was him knackered. That's what yer get for doing the right thing. He sofa surfed for a bit before he ran out of favours and friends. The world can be a lonely place, especially if yer on your arse. Yer find out who yer true friends are when it comes on top like that. People hate it when yer vulnerable, though, it makes 'em feel awkward and ashamed. So they attack. They invade. They abuse and take the total piss. Shocking how people can turn into bullies when confronted by weakness. And Johnner was weak and vulnerable coz he was nice and he cared. And people will just take advantage of that, won't they? All them scumbags in that hostel were skanking him left right and centre – money, meds, smokes, anything he had got taxed. Took advantage of him, they did, took advantage of his good nature. Vultures, they was.

So I looked after him. Too right, mate. Anyone tried to take the piss and I was straight up in their faces. He was gentle and placid and I looked after him. And he dint ask for owt back either, dint pester me for sex. I told him, I said I dint mind if he went off with other lasses as long as he stayed my friend. But he want interested in other lasses, he said. Said he just wanted to be with me. We cuddled up to keep warm and I'd kiss him sometimes when I'd had a drink, but that was as far as it went.

Anyway, neither of us had had a drink for weeks. Johnner couldn't anyway, not with them tablets he was on. It just made him sick as a dog.

Eventually, I went down to probation to see if anyone down there had seen him and this kid said he'd seen him arguing with some Polish lads near Queens Gardens first thing that morning. So I bombed across there and this other kid told me yeah, Johnner had been there and he'd had this kid pinned up against the wall and was proper going mad about summat; proper going off his head, and these other fellas had to get between them. And that's when I started to properly worry coz that was not like Johnner. Not like him one bit. I even asked this kid three times: Johnner? Johnner with the ginger dreads and the beard and green army jacket and the limp? Yeah, that's him, he said. Proper going off on one, he said.

I did all the usual rounds – St Mary's, down to Bev Road, on Spring Bank, round Pearson Park, up on Bankside, down Anlaby Road, Hessle Road and back into town again. I asked everyone I knew but nobody had seen sight nor sound of him.

No Johnner anywhere.

I went and planted meself on a bench back in Queens Gardens. There was no one there; no one I knew anyway. I tried not to think about things. I tried not cry. Can't remember the last time I'd cried – properly, I mean. Sweared down after I finally turned sixteen and got meself away from Him Who's Name I Will Not Say that I would not shed tears over nobody or nothing ever again. Certainly not over no man. I just felt horrible though, mate. Felt like an utter piece of shit. I really really wanted a drink an'all, for the first time in ages. Just wanted to get wrecked, smashed, fucked up to oblivion.

It was all just too much.

Every time, every bastard time yer get something nice and think yer getting somewhere, life just steams in and kicks yer in the guts; throws yer face down in the dirt and tramples all over yer. I got me photo of me girls out, me two beautiful angels who they snatched away from me, me photo of them all dressed up bonny in their matching tops and their hair done up in bunches and the tears started to come then. I couldn't help it, the tears just poured out of me...

– You alright, love?

I looked up and it was my nice woman in the white coat. I just shook my head and put me head down again. I dint want anyone being nice to me, no, fuck off, fuck off, just fuck off...

– What is it, love? Has someone been...?

I just jumped up and pushed past her, just got off. Dint need no pretty words, fuck off. Next thing I knew, I was coming out of Sainsbury's on Spring Bank with four cans of Karpackie.

When yer stop drinking and then yer start again, you get yer buzz back straight away. Bang, it hits yer like a lorry. Does with me, anyway. I'm no alkie; I can go without a drink for days – weeks, even. I can even buzz off not drinking, but when I'm back on it, I'm on it fucking proper, mate. Big time. I hate it. I hate it so much, but it's too easy, mate, it's far too easy.

I was sat on the wall drinking when Skinner rolled up with some of his cronies. Grinning all over his ugly little face, he was. I was just gonna get off. I want in the mood for his clever attitude, but he just come straight out with it:

– Ey, he says, – your Johnner's fucked, int he.

– What? I says to him. – What do yer mean? Why?

– Got taxed.

– Who did?

– Johnner. Some lads took his meds off him.

– What lads? Polish?

– No, these were local. Some little cunts off Bev Road. He come out the chemist and they just took 'em off him.

– What, yesterday?

– Yeah. When he got his prescription.

Horrible little bastard grinned at me. I wanted to punch his fucking lights out, but I was trying to stay calm.

– How do you know this?

– Coz he told us.

He turned to his little crew of no-marks. – Told us, dint he?

They all nodded and went yeah, told us, yeah.

– Who? Who told yer?

– Fucking *Johnner*.

– When?

– About an hour ago.

I tried to remember Johnner's face from yesterday. I dint remember seeing any new marks on him.

– What, and they just took 'em off him?

– Yer know what he's like, says Skinner. – Fucking dopey cunt, int he.

I could feel the anger shooting up me chest, but I swallowed it down. Tried to think. Trouble was, I'd sank three of them cans and I was pissed up by now.

– And yer've just seen him?

– About an hour ago, yeah.

21

– Where was he?

– Marching up and down here going mad. Said he was gonna stab these kids.

I felt proper, proper sick.

– Who are they?

– Just some little wannabes on mountain bikes. They all hang round in the carpark back of Lidl.

I just turned and set off running. Total blind panic. I nearly got knocked arse over tit by a car that was shooting out a side street, missed me by inches, slammed his brakes full on and blasted his horn at me, but I was off, mate. Full pelt up Spring Bank. I could hear someone shouting after me, but I dint stop, dint even look back.

At the top of Bev Road, I tripped and went flying, scraped all the palms of me hands and ripped the knee of me jeans, but I was straight back up and off again. Me head and every bit of me body was singing with pain, but I just kept running. Tunnel vision, mate. Pure adrenaline

I got to Lidl carpark; I dint see no kids, but there were two cop cars parked up with the blue lights turning and a big group of people stood round gawping. Summat serious had happened; you could feel it in the air. It was like everything had frozen, come to a full stop. This woman was stood with a trolley full of shopping, her hand held up to her mouth. She looked terrified. I pushed my way past her and there was this mountain bike on its side and a big black puddle on the floor and it was blood, I knew it was blood straight away. These two coppers were talking to some people in blue and yeller Lidl tops. This other copper was stood to one side, talking into his radio. I was straight on to him.

– What's happened, where is he? I says.

This copper turns round and looks at me. He says summat else into his radio and clips it onto his belt.

– Where is he? I'm going. – Where the fuck is he?

I'm proper freaked out by now, screaming in this copper's face. He holds his hands up, takes a step forward.

– Whoa, he says. – Whoa, whoa! Calm down!

He goes as if to grab me by the arm, but I jump back.

– Don't touch me, I says. – Do not fucking touch me.

– Just calm down, he's saying.

I go over to the group of people stood watching, the woman with the trolley.

– What happened? I ask her. She dunt say owt, just shakes her head. She looks at me like she's petrified of me.

– It was a mistake, I tell her. – They robbed his meds. It wunt have happened if they'd just left him alone. Why can't people just fucking leave us alone?

More people were coming out the shop, stopping, gathering round. I heard someone ask what's happened, what's going on?

– A lad got stabbed, someone said.

I look round. An old fella, white hair, glasses. He's looking at me like I got two fucking heads.

– What lad? I say. – Did you see it? What lad?

– I don't know, he says. – They took him off in an ambulance. One of them homeless, it looked like.

I've proper lost it now. I'm ranting away like a mad woman. He's not like that, I'm telling him; they robbed his meds. He goes funny if he dunt tek 'em. This old bloke is shaking his head and turning away like he doesn't want to know, but it's important that he listens. I need them to listen, all of them, I need them all to understand.

– Ey, do you mind? he says.

I realise I've got a hold of him by the jacket. I can see this copper coming for me so I let go and start back-pedalling. I'm still roaring and carrying on and this copper's saying OK, it's OK, calm down, let's just have a chat, trying to placate me like, but I know what he's after. I know his game. He's after cuffing me and getting me in the back of the car.

I took off.

They wunt let me see him at Infirmary. I knew exactly where he'd be, we'd both been there loads a times before. The lass on the desk told me she cunt give any personal details, blah blah blah, but yes, they had admitted a young man suffering from stab wounds and he was being operated on and who are you, please?

– I'm his girlfriend, I told her.

I'd managed to calm meself down a bit by then. She was looking me up and down. I could see she was itching to call security so I kept meself calm and composed and said if she dint mind, I'd wait and mebbe she could tell me how he was when they'd finished with him? Please, I said. Please.

She said she'd see what she could do.

So I sat there in Casualty on one of them hard plastic orange chairs for what seemed like forever. The days and nights I'd wasted in there. Usually a Friday or Saturday night, sat among a load of pissed-up lads and lasses fresh from battling round town. Or the serious street drinkers, the proper alkies, fallen over with broken wrists or smashed-in faces. Bandaged-up heads and stitches and the stink of chemicals and stale booze. Hours crawling by, watching them double-doors flap open, waiting to hear your name called. I remember that time when Johnner broke his ankle, back when we were both proper drinking, and he'd jumped off that wall in the playground in park the day before, just messing about, and he'd cockled over and started spewing up. No way did he wanna go to Infirmary, but I could tell it was serious by the way it swelled up all black and I was adamant he went. Nine hours we was in there.

I sat there for ages. The same news clips playing on the telly over and over again. Crowds of people in America chanting with signs and banners. Buildings and people and babies getting bombed in Syria. An aeroplane taking off. A footballer scoring a goal. Things were happening. The world outside turning. I cunt remember the last time I'd seen the news. I was waiting to see if that blade was gonna be on, all the performance they'd had putting it in and that. Seemed like a million years ago, that. The age of the dinosaurs. I started to wonder if I'd actually just dreamed it; if I'd go back in town and it would be gone, just an empty space in the square and nobody stood around looking up. I wondered if Johnner had seen it when he'd woken up and got off to look for them kids. Whether he'd noticed it, even. Probably wunt have. In a bastard daydream half the time, he was.

Johnner. You stupid, stupid twat, Johnner. Yer should have just told me. I'd have gone and sorted it. I'd have got 'em back for yer. I'd have looked after yer, mate.

Eventually, the girl on the desk came over and told me that they'd operated on him and it was a success and he'd had a blood transfusion and he was resting now and I should go home and they'd call me when I could come and see him.

– I don't have a phone, I told her.

– Well, come back tomorrow and we'll see how he is, she said. She smiled at me. She had a nice smile. She was nice, that lass. She dint call security or owt like that. She could have done, but she dint.

So I said, – Yeah, alright then, thank you. I'll come back tomorrow.

I hung about outside for a bit. I cadged a cig off this fella with one leg in a wheelchair who had booled himself over to the smoking zone. Must have been barmy, sat there in his dressing gown in that weather. It looked like it was gunna piss it down. The sky was starting to get dark. You could feel it in the air. I stood and had a cig with him and then I noticed people were going in with flowers and fruit and what have yer. Visiting time.

I went back in.

The security guard was at the far end chatting up the lass on the coffee bit, so I sloped across to where the lifts where and stood waiting with everyone else. The doors to one of the lifts opened and these two nurses stepped out.

– Excuse me, I said, – me boyfriend's just been operated on and I've forgot what floor he's on. He's just come out of surgery.

– What's he had done? one of them says.

– He's been stabbed, I tell her.

– Is it abdominal? she says.

– Yeah, I says. – I think so.

– Probably sixth floor, her mate says.

– Ta very much, I says.

I slip in the lift just before the doors close, along with the rest of the visitors and I get out at the sixth floor.

When I see him, I nearly walk straight back out again. He's fast asleep on his back with loads of tubes and wires coming out of him. Bags of fluid hung up and machines beeping and flickering. I wanted to pull the covers back and look at his belly but I dint want to disturb him. Half of me wanted to look and the other half dint.

– Johnner, I said. – Johnner. You shunt have broke the vow.

I dint know what to do.

I stayed there and talked to him and stroked his hair until the nurse came round and said everybody had to go. I told her what had happened, about him getting taxed and that she had to make sure he had some Tryptizol. That it was important he had his meds.

She said not to worry, she'd sort it out.

I went outside and stood looking up at the big yeller windows for a bit. Then I got para that the pigs would come looking for me, so I got off. I just kept walking. It got darker and darker. I avoided the places where I thought I'd see somebody I knew. I thought about going back to Lidl, back to the carpark, but I knew them kids wunt go back yet. But they would, eventually. And even if they dint, I'd find 'em.

I'd find 'em and I'd sort the bastards out.

It was proper night time when I got back to the square. There want hardly anybody about. All the shops had shut and the bluecoats were gone. The blade was still there. I walked underneath it, went right up to the big thick beginning bit and leaned back. It was hard and smooth against me shoulders. I was beyond tired. I knew it was all camera'd up round there, but I dint care. Not anymore. I shut me eyes, rested 'em just for a few seconds.

If I fell asleep it dint matter. Someone would come and move me before too long.

The Light That Lights The Dark

He gets up before you, goes downstairs and lays the table; a plate of toast with the margarine at two o'clock, the jam at three o'clock, a mug of tea on the right-hand side and the knife on the left. You sit and eat together and talk about the day ahead. He tells you that it looks like it's going to be a nice day outside and you should both go for a walk, blow away the cobwebs.

When you've finished breakfast, he runs you a bath and holds your hand as you step in. He washes and conditions and rinses your hair and then goes through to the bedroom and lays your clothes out on the bed from left to right: knickers, bra, fishnets, the long multi-layered black and mauve skirt, the black satin bustier, your favourite mesh top. Then he gets himself dressed and flicks through the TV channels until you call for him to help you out of the water.

And when you're dressed he blow-dries your hair, your head between your knees as the heat roars around your scalp. Then the backcombing, the gentle tugging and teasing of his fingertips and then the throat catching blasts of hairspray, the mist settling on your spikes like a sticky net. He sits you down in front of the mirror and does your make up. The cold lick of foundation and the tickle of the brush on your cheeks and forehead. He describes the colours he's using around your eyes, the purples and the greys and greens and then falls silent as he leans in closer and concentrates on drawing in the lines around your eyes, the arch of the brows and the cat lick at each corner, his warm breath at the side of your face.

I'm getting good at this, he says, and you say that you'll be the judge of that.

He paints your lips a congealed blood-red and then he helps you with your piercings; four in the left ear, five in the right, the bolt through the left eyebrow and the two fang-rings in your bottom lip. You sit before the mirror and he tells you that you look stunning and you know that he's telling you the truth because it's only been eight months now, not even a year, and the marks have all faded, but the memory of your own beauty has not.

You follow the banister downstairs and sit on the next-to-bottom step, prop your legs up on his lap, first one and then the other, feel the laces pull the leather together and the buckles tighten around your calves. You fasten up your coat and step outside the front door. The air is damp still, but you can feel the pale sunshine behind the clouds and you can smell the morning, fresh and clean and not yet ruined.

Looks like it's going to be a nice day, he says and you say yes, you've already said and you strive to keep the snap out of your voice because you know he's trying his best and it's not his fault, it's not his fault.

It wasn't his fault.

Take his arm and walk the fifty-four steps down the still quiet street and turn left onto the main road; more people and noise here, heavier traffic, streams of exhaust fumes with each passing vehicle. You feel the weight and swiftness of their passing and you cannot help but lean into him, fasten your fingers more tightly around his arm.

Pass the row of shops and know each one in turn; Blooming Lovely, its damp dark greenness overlaid with soft rosy pinks and milky whites and the sharp primrose yellows that sing out spring; the fresh metallic tang of Len Fletcher Family Butcher, your nostrils flaring at the hint of blood; TopKnotz and the harsh chemical hit of scrubbed hands and cheap setting lotion, a row of middle-aged women in the window, reading magazines and balancing cups of teas on their laps, their heads bagged or crowned with rollers. Then no obvious smells at all as you pass the open door of PoundLand and the closed glass frontages of the Estate Agents and the Opticians, before you come to the Indian And Continental Store and you can almost taste the heavy notes of cinnamon and ginger and turmeric and star anise and you hear a hello from the young man who forever leans in the doorway watching the world go by and you turn your head to his voice and smile hello back. Then the sudden citrus zing of Fruitopia where you stop to pick up fruit, your thumb rubbing the waxy pock-marked orange spheres, the rubbery clumps of grapes and the solid heft of the apples; you feel their weight as they drop into the paper bag he holds open at your elbow.

You wait outside while he pays and you hear a high pitched whine of machinery from further down along the street, the laughter of men above tinny pop music. He comes back out of the shop with the fruit and you ask him what's going on and he tells you that it looks like they're knocking through the two shut-down shops at the end of the row, looks like a new bar or restaurant, he says. One of those trendy café-bar affairs where lads in short-sleeved shirts and girls in too-small dresses huddle under glowing orange gas burners and pretend they're on the continent. Looks like all the others down here, he says.

Sometimes he tries to describe everything that's going on around you, and on a good day you are happy to let him talk, knowing it's his way of trying to make everything more normal, for himself as well as you. But today is not a good day for you; last night's sleep broken by bad memories; sharp black shadows falling across patches of dappled sunlight, scuffed trainers and bare torsos, rough voices and leering eyes and now him droning on and on about bland piped music and shabby chic and the cultural hegemony of the middle-classes and you tell him to shut the fuck up, please, the slur in his voice like a wet mop dragging across your nerves. You tell him you can still remember what the fucking bars are like, it's been eight months not eight fucking years. And he clams up, chastised, and you don't need to see his face to know what it's doing. The tight-lipped mouth and clenched jaw – you can feel it in the weight of his silence and the quickening of his pace as he pulls you along the street and you tell him to slow down, please, that's enough, leave him alone, fucking leave him you set of bastards you're hurting

(no)

He adjusts his pace to an exaggerated stroll and you feel bad for snapping at him because it's not his fault, it wasn't his fault, and you try to make small talk, but he barely responds, just hmms and yeps and suppose so's through a buttoned up mouth and you feel the tension in the crook of his elbow and you think this cannot go on, we are letting them win.

31

So you take a deep breath and say you want to go to the park and feed the ducks and he doesn't reply and you know that his Adam's apple is bobbing up and down in his throat like a tiny drowning man and you sense the sudden wave of fear that washes over him, can smell it almost, and this frustrates you further.

What had Tara called it in the Therapy Sessions? Mutual Reinforcement. Mutual Reinforcement is very important, she'd said. There are things that each of you can do that the other cannot. Any successful partnership is based on balance and exchange; your optimism for his caution, your gut instinct for his logic, your mental strength for his timidity. We need to work together to confront our fears, she said. We can't let them stop us doing the things we always used to do. We have to move forward, not allow the past to anchor us down. We can't let them win, she'd said. She had annoyed you at first, Tara, with her voice of carefully adopted encouragement and her textbook terminology, her talk of *emotional restructuring* and *incremental advancement*. But you recognize the hard kernel of truth behind the cotton wool words and in your heart, you know that this cannot go on.

I want to go to the park, you tell him. I want to feed the ducks and sit down at the plastic tables and have an ice cream from the hut, a 99 with hundreds and thousands and sticky red syrup. You remember the Whitby weekends with Storm and Fury and Olivia and the rest of the clan; the pints of snakebite in the sunshine and the Dracula cones, licking blackcurrant and liquorice sauce off your fingers. The locals were used to you and your twice-yearly descents, but the straight-head day trippers from Yorkshire and Teesside would stare with open mouths and bemused shakes of the head at your lace and leather and full face make-up, their eyes lingering in horrified fascination or dismissing with sneering bemusement. And you enjoyed the stares and the sneers because you were proud and unified and strong and their revulsion could not touch you, could only make you stronger.

You say let's go to Maria's and get some stale bread for the ducks. And he says yes OK, and your heart leaps and you reach down for his hand and squeeze it tight and you both turn to cross the road, walking in step together again until you feel the raised bumps at the pavement edge beneath your boots and you wait for the beep-beep-beep of the pelican crossing and the idling of the engines.

And you walk in pregnant silence until you turn and push open a door and the next voice you hear is Maria's; Ah! Bella, she says, Bella Signora! It is my bonny lass! That sing-song accent caught halfway between Hull and Sicily. You put your hip against the counter and you feel the hot blast of breath from the opening ovens, fresh bread and garlic and rosemary and you say hiya Maria, how are you? And you throw a hello somewhere over to the back of the shop, where you hear the faintest Ciao Bella from Freddie, his greetings getting weaker with the last few passing weeks, you've noticed, but your image of him still vivid and clear, him sat in his chair by the doorway to the back room, his hands folded upon the top of his stick, those slow-moving brown eyes and tired smile. Ciao Bella, he says.

You buy almond and orange biscuits and a bag of stale ciabatta and you set off towards the park, him talking again, pointing out people you know and points of interest and anything, anything to quell the nerves you both feel, the sickness blooming from the pit of your stomach and

33

your legs turning to water and your fingernails digging into the leather of his sleeve. You hear the distant noise of children yelling and you remember that it's half-term and the playground will be full and there will be people, normal people, mams and dads and granddads and nanas and not just gangs of lads with baseball caps and cans of lager and crudely inked skin and sneering mouths and voices scorched by glue and cheap alcohol and cigarettes and fuck me lads look at the state of this pair of fucking weird cunts

(no)

and you think it will be OK, it will be OK, it will be OK; this world is not totally dark and rotten to the core, there is sunshine and innocence and the laughter of children, there are swings and slides and roundabouts and ducks and ice creams and what are you then love a fucking vampire

(no no no)

You push down the mounting panic as you turn into the park; the rush of water from the fountain, the fine mist of its spray on the side of your face as you approach the edge of the pond, the reek of yellowing scum on the surface. He breaks the bread and passes you handfuls and you cast them out onto the water, remembering the ducks and how they would come gliding across towards the bobbing scraps of white and then the sudden flap of pigeons descending from the treetops and the frantic honking of the Canadian geese crowding around your fingertips and knees as they jostle for the food, the heavy brush of wing and snap-snap-snap of beaks and give us a fucking kiss then love fucking joking aren't yer don't kiss that Jacko you'll get fucking Aids

(no no no no no)

You throw the last handfuls of the bread as hard as you can, as far away as you can, and the clamour of the geese recedes as they turn tail and chase, bumping against your legs, fighting past each other for the final crumbs and you try to resist the overwhelming urge to turn and run and where the fuck do you think you're going you freaky fucking bitch

(NO!)

His hand on your arm and you reach for him, take tight hold and he says shall we go and see George in the Conservatory, it should be open if the kids are off and you say yes, yes, the conservatory, let's go and see George and he leads you away from the pond, across the flower garden; quieter here, calmer, the sudden burst of colour in your nostrils and the wind slowly swaying the heavy tree branches twenty feet above your head.

And then the thick wet warmth of the Victorian conservatory, the heavy musk of vegetation, the chatter and whistles from the aviary and the gentle drip-drip-drip from the freshly watered hanging baskets that line the walkway.

He leads you down to George and tells you he's going to look at the tarantulas and you say yes you do that and he leaves you there, your heart gradually slowing back down, the palms of your hands against the cage, the tiny squares of metal pressed into your flesh and the heat from the lamp on your face and you remember how beautiful George is, those tightly balled muscles beneath that glistening grey-green skin, those lazy lidded eyes and flickering tongue, those claws like little swords gripping onto his branch, sat there silently and never stirring from one day to the next.

35

You stay and talk to George for a while until he comes back from the spider tank and touches your neck and says, how about one in the Polar Bear? I think we deserve it, he says, and you agree yes we do, and you both say goodbye to George and you hold that image of him, his calm unmoving stoicism, take it back out of the Conservatory and across the flower garden, past the pond and out of the park and down the road to the Polar Bear where you take your seat in the corner next to the jukebox and say hello to Mad Sally and Sid and the Harpic Brothers, the regulars who gravitate towards your table in the hope of companionship and drinks bought from your compensation money, but you don't mind about that, because these are your favourite kind of people; the eccentric and the dispossessed, the day-time drinkers who trade tall tales and friendly insults and do not judge on looks or chosen lifestyle, as long as there are drinks and stolen cigarettes and raw and raucous laughter.

You sit and sip cider and black and listen to the jukebox and the click of the pool balls, the friendly bedlam of the bar, and you feel warm and safe and secure and you lean in close and whisper to him I think we did well there, and he whispers back yes, we'll tell Tara on Monday, she'll be pleased won't she and you say oh yes, proper breakthrough moment that wasn't it, she'll probably write a fucking dissertation about it and you both laugh and laugh until the tears stream down your cheeks and Mad Sally says you're bloody barmy you two. And you stay there in the pub laughing and drinking and talking until the lunch time turns to late afternoon and you can feel the sun moving across the big bay windows and almost see the dust dancing in the stripes of sunlight that slant through onto the beer-stained floor.

Sometimes you think you can make things out; flashes of light in your peripheries, blurred shapes and movement like quick grey clouds rolling across a sky at dusk and this causes you to catch your breath and wait for it to pass. And sometimes you flinch at the touch of a helping hand or an unexpected voice at your side, especially if the voice is young and male.

Their names were Callum Munroe, Lee Beadle, Anthony John Jackson, Scott Fleming and Colin White; four of them charged with Section 18 assault and sentenced to three years in a Young Offenders Unit, all except Jackson, who continued after the others had fled and was charged with attempted murder and imprisoned for an indeterminate period for public protection, such was the sustained nature of his attack, launching kick after kick, long after you had both lost consciousness and stopped moving.

And the letter two months ago from Jackson, addressed to you both by name and passed onto Tara by Humberside Police and Tara asking if you'd like her to read it aloud and you said yes, yes please and the both of you sat there holding hands and listening to her voice, calm and steady and neutral, and behind that the surly mumbling of Anthony John Jackson, and behind that the voices of the Probation Officer and Social Worker and Prison Chaplain, prompting and abetting when the writer struggled for the appropriate words of remorse as if words could ever truly say sorry or piece together the fragile fragments that actions had smashed apart. And Tara not a quarter of the way through this pitifully staged apology before you were up on your feet, the chair fallen backwards behind you, hand clamped over your mouth to stop the vomit spraying her desk.

But that has been pushed away to a corner of your mind, dropped into the box marked do not disturb and you are pleased with today and the strength you have shown.

So you go home together and he cooks the tea and you eat together from trays on your lap in front of the TV and you listen to the news and then later you play Nick Cave and drink Rioja until bed time, when he takes the make-up off your face and helps you to undress and take out your piercings before you get into your pyjamas.

He reads to you in bed, the book you had started eight months ago, the one about the Scottish girl who woke up one morning to find her boyfriend dead on the kitchen floor and he reads until his voice becomes tired and his slurring turns the words to mush in his mouth and you say OK that's enough, let's go to sleep. And you bury yourself beneath the quilt and he tells you he is going to keep the light on so he can read some more and you say yes, OK, and your toes reach out and rub up and down his leg.

You lay awake and listen to the turning of his pages until he puts down his book and goes to the bathroom, his footsteps retreating down the landing, then the long splashing of his piss and the flush of the toilet, the quick burst of the taps and then his footsteps returning and the weight of him getting back into bed, the click of the light turning off.

Night-night, God Bless, he whispers, and you feel his bristles on the side of your face as he kisses you goodnight and then settles himself down. You lay there in the black of the room and you listen to him breathing, waiting for the darkness of sleep.

A Circus Poster On A Chinese Wall

Me Dad's having chicken balls. Uncle Terry wants that beef thing that he likes; beef with black bean sauce. Me Mam says she's not bothered.

– Number seventy-three with fried rice, not boiled, and a carton of curry sauce. Number fifty-eight with chips. And a bag of prawn crackers, please.

Terry says I can have what I want with the change. He means curry and chips or summat, but I'm not eating any more Chinky. Bollocks to that. I'm proper sick of it. One pound eighty-four change. That's going straight in my pocket, that is. There's three people waiting for their orders in front of me, a woman and two blokes. I go and sit down near the window. It's all steamed up. I write HCAFC and JASE in big dripping letters.

It's always busy in here. It's the best Chinese on Holderness Road, me Dad reckons. Me Mam says they all taste the same to her; says she can't tell the difference between this one and any other. I reckon me Dad only thinks this is the best one coz it's the nearest. It's alright though, the Golden Dragon. At least it's clean and they have the telly on. Sometimes it's a lad and his little sister serving. The little lass is ace. She stands up on this stool behind the counter with a pad and a pen and a proper solemn face, like she's taking her job dead serious. The lad goes to my school. He's called Michael Zhang. He's in our year, but I don't talk to him. He's not a dickhead or owt; he just knocks about with different people. He's not here now though, and neither is his sister. It's the woman on tonight. I think she must be the mam. She looks old enough to be the mam. I reckon she's at least thirty-five, thirty-six. It's hard to tell sometimes with Chinese people. She's dead fast at sorting out the orders, though. They pass her the trays through that sliding hatch and she has them all wrapped and bundled and bagged up in ten seconds flat. It's brilliant how she does it. The cartons stay hot all the way home and make the plastic bag go all wet inside.

I don't know how they can eat this stuff all the time. They've had it every night for the past four nights. Saturday, they all went out for a drink and brought a massive takeaway back, tons of it there was. It was all over the kitchen the next morning still. They hadn't even bothered to scrape their plates into the bin. Cartons of cold red glop, bleurgh. It was proper rank. Sunday, they were rowing, so me Mam wouldn't do any cooking. Last night, I went for some chips after school and now tonight me Uncle Terry's come round with a load of cans to watch the football with me Dad. So I've been sent out here again. I'm not having Chinese, though. No way. I'm getting them this and then I'm off out. I'll go to Maccy D's and then call for Albo. I'm not staying in and watching football with that dickhead.

Football's shit, anyway. I used to play on a Sunday, but I can't be arsed now. It's too much of an effort. Besides, I grew out of me boots, and me Mam says it's too dear to

get a new pair. Or the pair I want, anyway. I wanted some
Nike Hypervenoms, but they're about fifty quid. She says
why don't you just get some off eBay? Yeah, right. As if.
An old knackered second-hand pair of boots that
someone's already ragged to bits. Adidas Saddo. I'm not
bothered, though. I've jacked it in anyway. There were too
many wankers. In the end there was, anyhow, especially
them Prentons. They've totally ruined that team, them
and their knob-head of a dad. Just coz he sponsored the
new strip he thinks that gives him the right to stick his
oar in and order everyone about. He even tried to tell
Coach Ron how to set up the back four when we were
getting battered by Hall Road Rangers the other week. He
wrote it all out on a bit of paper and handed it to Coach
Ron at halftime. Coach Ron looked at it and said yeah,
we'll maybe give it a go, Barry. But I could tell he just
wanted him to butt out and stop interfering. Like that
other time before, when he caused that massive kick off
on the touchline and all coz that winger kept going past
their Gary. Gary's too slow to play fullback; everyone
knows that, the fat little barrel. This little winger was
skinning him every time and we were three nil down after
about twenty minutes, all the goals coming down Pudding
Prenton's side. His dad was going mental on the
touchline, screaming and bawling at me and Macca to get
back and help their Gary. As if it's our fault the fat little
twat can't play football. He can't even run properly. He
runs like a girl; like a chubby little lass. He's even got tits
like a lass. Anyway, his dad caused mayhem by grabbing
hold of this winger's shirt. He reckoned he'd knocked it
out as he was dribbling along the line. The linesman's flag
stayed down but Prenton's old man was going mental,
swinging this kid around by the scruff of his neck. This

41

other dad came steaming over and it all kicked off; nose-to-nose they was, screaming and bawling, pushing each other about. Coach Ron and Big Les had to separate them. It was proper ace. But Coach Ron was fuming afterwards. He threatened Prenton's dad with a touchline ban but the big gobby bastard was still there the next Sunday, larging it on the touchline, giving it the big I am.

I wish she'd hurry up with this food. It's boring just sat here waiting. The match is on the telly behind the counter, but the screen's tiny and the sound's turned down so you can't hear it properly anyway. City are in their purple away strip. I don't rate it. They look weird when they're not in amber and black. We used to play in red until Mr Prenton bought that new strip. Now we're in green and white coz that's the colours of his business. It even says it on the front of the shirts: PRENTON AUTOS in big green letters.

Very professional, lads. That's what he said when he handed them out at training. He shouldn't have even been allowed at training. I didn't think they looked professional. I thought they looked shit. What decent team plays in green and white? Only Celtic, and they're Scottish so they don't count. Albo reckons he's gonna go and work for Prenton's when we leave next year. Says he's gonna be a motor mechanic. Says he can do an apprenticeship and the firm gets some sort of grant off the government and him and Prenton's dad are gonna go halves on the money. I wouldn't work for Prenton if he paid me a hundred quid a week. Anyway, bollocks to the lot of 'em. I'm jacking it. Jacked it, in fact. Done deal.

There's a poster on the wall next to where I'm sat. There's a circus coming. In June, it says. That's miles off. It looks crap. It's not even a proper photo; just a drawing.

There's a picture of a stupid grinning clown and a woman in a glittery bikini with feathers in her hair and a picture of a big top, red and yellow stripes. Big wow. There's a bloke breathing fire as well, all the flames shooting out of his gob, but there's no tigers or monkeys or owt like that. No elephants. I think it's meant to be cruel now to have animals in a circus. I don't agree with that, personally. If you can have animals in a zoo or a safari, why can't you have them in a circus? Doesn't make sense. Why have one rule for one and not the other? It's just political correctness. That's why my Dad can't get a job, coz they give them out to all the asylum seekers and the Kosovans and the people who haven't been here five minutes.

It's gonna be in East Park, this circus. It'll be on the main field, where they had the *Party In The Park*. That was ace that was. I wasn't arsed about the bands, but all the food stalls and the massive crowds and the fireworks at the end was ace. My Dad reckons he's gonna get a burger van if they do it next year. Licence to print money, he says. Maybe he can get one lined up for when this circus comes. Unless they bring their own vans, like they do with Hull Fair. I don't know how it works with circuses. If he can get a burger van, I'll go and work on it with him. We'll go halves on the money. Maybe even get enough for some Hypervenoms. I'll start playing again if I get some decent boots.

I saw me Mam and me Uncle Terry on East Park last year. That was when I first found out. Last summer it was, just before we broke up from school. A load of us went on the big field to play football. Normally when we twag we go round to Leon's house coz his mam and dad are both at work, but this day it was miles too hot to stay inside on the Xbox and that, so we went on park and larked football.

43

We were all lying around on the grass afterwards and someone said hey Jase, that's your mam, innit?

And it was. It was her and me Uncle Terry at the far side of the field, going past the bandstand and into that bit where that little ornamental pond is; that little secret garden bit that's behind all the big hedges. I saw them going through the entrance. It was about two o'clock, half two, and the game was finished. Everyone was drifting off home or wherever, so I said ta-ra to the lads and made out like I was getting off.

I walked across to the entrance to the gardens but instead of going through, I followed the hedge all the way round to the other side. I know where there's a gap that brings you out behind this old shed. We used to use it to ambush people when we were larking war when we were little. I ran round the other side of the bushes and crept through this gap. I was stood behind this old shed and they were there, on the other side of the pond. They were sat on one of the benches. I could see them. There was no one else around. Me Uncle Terry was just sat there like he didn't know what to do and me Mam was crying. I couldn't hear any noise or owt, but I could tell she was crying coz she had her face in her hands and her shoulders were going up and down. Our Terry tried to put his arm around her, but she pulled away. He did it another two times. Then he put his head near hers and they started talking, but I couldn't hear what they were on about. I could tell it was a serious talk, though. After a bit, me Mam stood up and he stood up as well and this time she let him put his arms around her. She let him put his arms *properly* around her and he pulled her close and kissed her on the top of the head and then he lifted her face up and kissed her on the mouth. She kissed him back as well. Full mouth. I saw it.

I saw everything.

That night, when we were having our tea, I said to me Mam, – Mam, did Sheila do owt funny at work today?

There was this woman she worked with who was always doing mad things and saying mad things to the customers and me Mam used to tell us about her.

– Not today, she said, – no.

– Was it good at work today then? I said. I said it real casual.

– It was alright, said Mam, but then she changed the subject. – Use your knife properly, please, she said. – Hold it like a human being; you're not a monkey in a zoo.

And that's when I knew.

City have scored. Snodgrass, free kick. A right cracker, as well. Bang, get in, straight in the top corner. Pick that one out. He turns and runs straight for the corner flag, plants a big kiss on the camera so his face fills up the entire telly screen. Brilliant goal.

I bet *his* boots didn't come off fucking eBay.

The hatch slides across and the trays of food are passed through and the woman wraps them up and puts them into a bag.

– Chicken balls, beef in black bean, fried rice, chips, curry sauce, prawn cracker.

That's me. I jump up to the counter and get the order and I run all the way home. I go in the back way and dump the hot bags on the kitchen table. There's no one in the kitchen, but I can hear loud voices from the living room. I can hear me Dad and me Uncle Terry shouting. I think they're just shouting at the telly. City must have scored again. Or the other team.

45

I don't know where me Mam is. She won't be in there with them, though. I know that for a fact. She can't even stand football.

Slowly

Louise is thinking about Kevin and what she's going to say to him when she gets to the pub. There are certain things she wants to happen. She is going to look him square in the eye and say them. She's not going to let him talk over her or bully her into stuff she doesn't want to do. She knows exactly what she wants to say and how she wants to say it. Calm. Measured. Firm. Not letting her voice crack. Not getting upset. She goes through everything in her head as she walks.

One o'clock in The Avenue. Cards on the table, they'd said. Get things sorted, once and for all.

She has her eyes on the pavement and doesn't notice the old lady up ahead until she nears the junction where Salisbury Street meets Westbourne. At first, Louise thinks the old lady is stood still, but as she gets closer she can see that she is indeed moving, but slowly, stopping every two or three small steps to lean on her stick. Louise can hear muttering as she draws level.

– Oh dear... oh dear me, what a game. What a bloody game.

– You alright, love?

The old lady looks around herself, flustered. Then she sees Louise at her elbow.

– Oh, do you know? says the old lady.

47

Her coat is unbuttoned and her legs are bare beneath her knee-length skirt. She wears fur-lined brown slippers split at the sides. It is early March and cold still, the last faint cobwebs of frost stuck to the pavement.

– Are you OK, love? Louise asks her.

– Well, I thought I'd do a spot of shopping, says the old lady. – But I've had to come back. I don't think I can manage.

She leans on her stick and twists herself around as if she is searching for someone. Then she looks up at Louise again. Her cheeks are touched cold with points of pink. Her eyes are rheumy and wet behind her glasses.

– The house, she says. – I should get meself back.

– Where do you live? Louise asks her.

– Oh, now then, yes... Thoresby Terrace. Do you know it?

– Off Thoresby Street?

The old lady puts her hand to her mouth.

– Oh, now hang on... yes. Off Thoresby Street, yes. Yes, it will be, won't it?

Thoresby. Nip across the road, left and then first right down to the Dukeries, past the Chinese and the hairdressers and the Mini-Mart and the primary school on the corner. Thoresby Street, the last street on the end. Not that far.

Louise looks at her watch: half past twelve. The Avenue is on the main road, in the opposite direction completely. But she has time.

– Here you are, she says. – I'll see you across the road.

She offers her arm.

– Oh, do you mind? Oh, you are good.

The old lady switches the stick to her other hand, and clings on to the crook of Louise's elbow. Louise puts her fingers over the old lady's knuckles and rubs them gently.

– Ooh, you're nithered! she says. – Come on, let's get that coat buttoned up.

Louise fastens her coat, then offers her arm again.

– Come on, let's get you home, love.

Louise looks left, right and then left again. There is nothing coming either way. – Here we go then, she says, and they step carefully down into the road. The old lady's fingers tighten on Louise's arm. Louise can sense the total surrender, the giving over. The tiny tremors of panic.

– You're alright, says Louise, – I've got you.

They move together across the road, slowly. Louise has to make a conscious effort to check her natural pace. She doesn't want the old lady to feel as though she is being hurried. It's difficult, though. She has to allow the old lady four or five tiny shuffling steps before she can make a single one of her own. Normally she'd be across this road in, what, three seconds flat? This is strange. And difficult. It takes a concerted effort to walk this slow.

They inch their way across. It seems to take an age. For one brief moment, Louise imagines picking the old lady up, just picking her up bodily and carrying her across the road like a child. She could do it. The old lady feels as light and as fragile as a bird. Like a sparrow has landed on her arm. Louise remembers reading somewhere that birds have hollow bones to help them glide upon the air. Light as a feather, she thinks. A sudden gust of wind and she'd be lifted up from her slippers and carried away over the rooftops. Louise folds her hand tightly over the old lady's fingers, feels them grip her sleeve in response.

A large silver people-carrier car emerges from a side street. The indicator flashes orange as it turns into the Avenue and rolls towards them. Louise and the old lady are about three feet into the road. If the two of them stopped dead on the spot, the car could pass in front of them, a comfortable distance away. Louise stops and waves the car on, but it is slowing right down, stopping, now waiting. The woman at the wheel fiddles with her phone, eyes down.

– Oh, I do hate to be a pain. I am sorry.

– You're not being a pain. Don't be silly...

The woman in the car glances up and then down again, continues sliding and tapping.

The next time she looks up, Louise and the old lady are about halfway across the road, just drawing level with the bumper of her car. The woman puts her phone away, turns the radio up and places both hands on the wheel, drumming her fingers.

Louise and the old lady shuffle forward. Louise smiles, mouths an apology and gets a thin-lipped smile in return.

As they near the opposite kerb, the car moves forward. Louise can feel the vibration of the vehicle passing behind them. The old lady's fingers fumble for a renewed grip, fasten harder.

– Oh, I am sorry, she says.

They get to the other side. They stand for a minute as the old lady gets her breath. The pavement leads around the corner, into the Dukeries and down to Thoresby Street. No more wide roads to cross. Thoresby Terrace is on the right-hand side as you walk down, the third or fourth terrace along. Not that far away. Louise thinks about leaving her here. The pub. Kevin. But the old lady isn't letting go.

– Will you be alright from here, love?

– Will Maureen be in?

– Who's Maureen?

– She'll have the key... if she's not in I'll be snookered.

– Who's Maureen, love? Is that your neighbour?

The old lady looks up and down the street, agitated; mutters words that Louise cannot hear.

– I beg your pardon? Louise leans in to listen. – What did you say, love?

The old lady looks at Louise and seems surprised to see her, as if she had forgotten she was there.

– Oh, I am sorry, she says. – What a pain I am.

The mobile vibrates in Louise's jacket. She takes it out and looks at it: KEVIN. The digits above his name read 12:45. Oh bloody hell, Kevin! For God's sake! One o'clock, they'd said. She hits DECLINE and slips the phone back into her pocket.

– Come on love, let's get you home.

He'll be in the pub, waiting. At least two empty pint glasses on the table by now. Getting more and more agitated. Kevin was always early for everything. On time, he called it. Whenever they went anywhere – going out for a drink, going shopping, anywhere – he'd be stood showered and changed and ready at the front door, fiddling with his phone, tapping his foot, jangling coins in his trouser pocket while she was still upstairs, drying her hair or getting dressed, or in the kitchen looking for her keys or her purse, panicking. Then he'd be stood behind her when they got back, sighing and tutting as she fumbled to get the key in the lock. Always hurrying her up. Always trying to set the pace. But who put him in charge? What gave him the right?

That Saturday night when she'd finally found the courage to ask him to leave. Even then, she couldn't be the one deciding. Not splitting up, he'd said. Trial separation. Control freak, that's what he was. Had to dictate everything. Set the agenda. That wasn't the reason she wanted to split, not really, but it was definitely part of it. It was a... what was the word? Factor? No, not factor. Too simple. Symptom. That's what it was, a symptom. Like they were both ill, like they had a disease and neither of them realised.

She'll tell him that. That will be one of the things she'll say.

– Terry won't be in. He'll be in pub.

– Who's Terry, love?

– Always in pub on a Saturday. He's entitled to a drink, though. Works hard.

– Is Terry your husband?

– Oh yes. Fifty-four years.

– Aw, that's nice.

Louise tries to think of something else to say. A distant roar swells up from beyond the rooftops. The football. City at home. Kevin had said something about that, something about an early kick off. Football should be at three o'clock, he'd said. Sky TV, it was all their fault.

– Does Terry go to football?

– He used to.

– Yeah, my husband's the same.

Her husband. She'd stopped thinking of him like that a long time ago. Partner. Other half. Husband. Hearing the word said out loud seemed wrong. It felt wrong in her mouth. Like swearing, almost.

– It's expensive as well now, isn't it?

– Oh, I don't know. I don't go. I expect it is, yes. My hus... Kevin, he hasn't been for ages. Says the owner's a bugger. Well, he used a different word to that, but still... always someone else's fault, though, isn't it? What about your Terry? Does he still bother?

– Who?

– Your husband. Does he still go to watch City?

– Oh no, he's dead.

– Oh, says Louise.

Two young lads on bikes heading towards them on the pavement. Louise stops and holds tight on to the old lady's arm as they sail past them, one on either side. The lad nearest to the kerb bunny-hops into the road and shouts something to his pal. Louise waits a few seconds, looks behind her to make sure they've gone before starting to move again.

– Little buggers. Should be on the road.

Louise tries to think of something else to say. Like, oh I am sorry about your husband. Or, how long has he been dead? But everything that comes to mind sounds wrong or silly. She can't think of anything else to say, so she concentrates on the few metres of frosted pavement ahead of them. One step at a time. There is a spread of broken glass, the remnants of a smashed vodka bottle in the gutter. The lad on the bike must have jumped into the road to avoid it. She considers moving to the other side of the old lady, swapping arms, but it seems too complicated a manoeuvre to negotiate. Instead, she stops and points to the ground.

– Mind that glass, she says.

They side-step slowly around the glinting shards, Louise acutely aware of the old lady's bare feet in those busted slippers. She looks closely for any stray lumps or fragments.

– Someone should clean that up. Disgraceful! Could cut yourself to ribbons on that!

She and Kevin were splitting up. Not a temporary thing, not a trial separation – final. Forever. She was sure about that. Her mind was made up. She tried to think what had taken her so long. Fear, probably. The fear of being alone. Forty-six wasn't old, not really. But it felt too old to start again. That was probably why she'd been putting this off. But the more she thought about it, the more Louise realised that she didn't want to start again. A month. That's what they'd said. What Louise had agreed to. And now, a month later, she knew that it wasn't long enough. She'd been lonely on her own in the house, true. But she'd been feeling lonely for months. Years, even. It had been years, when she thought about it. But being lonely on your own was better than being lonely with someone else.

Louise doesn't want to start again.

– How long has he been gone? Your Terry?

– Oh, a long time...

They arrive at the corner of Belvoir Street. The Mini-Mart on the opposite side of the road. Louise feels the pulsing of the mobile again in her jacket pocket. Can almost hear his voice – what you doing? Where are you? I've been here ages. Get a move on, for fucks sake. She fumbles down into her pocket and finds the off button, presses down hard with her thumb. Feels the power drain away.

– Did you get your shopping?

She remembers that the old lady had come out for some shopping. She didn't have any bags with her. She must have walked straight past the shop, poor old bugger. In a world of her own.

The old lady replies that she is OK love, she's OK. Louise tries to engage her further – the weather, the telly, what she's having for her tea. But it is difficult to establish a connection. The old lady's attention drifts away. Sentences begin and then evaporate into unfinished fragments. Louise asks her if she has any sons or daughters around here and she says yes, oh yes, I've got three... one of them high up at Needlers, she says. Oh, you'll be alright for chocolates, then, says Louise. Then she remembers that Needlers closed down years ago.

God, she thinks, what if I lose my mind and I'm on my own?

Moving so slowly, time becomes bigger. Empty spaces stretch out in front of you. You have to fill them with something. Louise starts to think about the things she needs to establish with Kevin. He has to move out permanently. That's number one. No, number one is that they are over. That they are finished. The marriage is finished. That's the first thing she has to say. Louise had practiced saying it out loud back home in the bedroom, sat on the edge of the bed, looking across an imaginary pub table, looking into his eyes and saying the actual words out loud – I want a divorce. But that word was too dangerous. If Kevin heard divorce he'd sink his teeth in even harder. It would give him something to fight against. Terms and conditions. Meetings. Sorting things out. Things to be negotiated.

I want this to finish.

That would be better.

That's what she'd say.

They pass the Mini-Mart and shuffle on slowly along Hardwick Street. More swells of noise from the stadium. The crowd are singing. Louise thinks she can recognise the melody. Some hymn or ancient song she sung at school. Kumbaya, my Lord, kumbaya. Was that it? She rubs the old lady's knuckles and places her own hand over them.

– Nearly there, she says.

– I hope Maureen's there.

The old lady shoots Louise a sudden frightened glance.

– She will be there, won't she?

– I would imagine so. She'll know you're coming back, won't she?

– Well, I don't know... I hope she's not gone out.

Louise suddenly realises that she doesn't know the old lady's name.

– What's your name, love? she asks. But the old lady has gone away again. She's staring across the street at the doors of the houses.

– Who lives there, then? she murmurs.

– I don't know, love, says Louise.

Second thing she needs to say is that she wants no contact. No phone calls, no popping round. Someone had told Louise that you have to have at least six clear months of daylight between you and your ex. Not all this hanging about and vague messy edges. There have to be boundaries. New markings. Lines drawn in the sand.

And there isn't anybody else. That will be the first conclusion he jumps to, but it's true. She doesn't even want anyone else. She has no interest. She wishes he would, though. Find someone else. That would make things infinitely easier. A proper six month break will enable him to do that. Get yourself a bird, Kevin. She won't say that, though. He would just twist it around, say that she was only saying that because that's what *she* wanted to do.

This is why it was important to keep it simple. So: marriage must end. *They* must end. Finished. No more Kevin and Louise. That's number one. Number two is no further contact. What was number three? Things worked best in threes. Didn't she have a number three? Something to do with money? Something practical like that? But no, it wasn't money. They'd kept separate bank accounts in the ten years they'd lived together. There were things she paid for and things he paid for, but nothing really in both their names. No loans, nothing outstanding. The bills, maybe. She thought maybe the gas was in his name and the electric in hers. But that was nothing; that could be dealt with. He'd have to find a flat, yeah, but that was no problem. He earned good money. He could stay where he was for a bit, at his mate's who was on the rigs. Rattling about in that big empty house by himself. Fell on his feet, there.

There was something else she had to say. The third thing.

She can't think what it is.

Instead, she tries to remember when she'd started to feel like this. Her friends had struggled to see anything wrong. What, you and Kevin? they'd said. We had no idea. What's the problem? And she couldn't really tell them. He didn't go out drinking all the time, didn't take drugs. He hadn't been unfaithful – not that she knew of, anyway. He didn't bray her. He brought home a decent wage. Got on fine with her kids. Kevin was always the confident one, always loud and laughing, cracking jokes, getting the drinks in. Always organising holidays and days out and

Christmas and what have you. And his hands had been all over that house. Soon after moving in, he'd re-decorated all the living room and bedroom. Bought new furniture. Fixed that leak in the downstairs toilet.

This last month on her own had been strange, yes, but she felt like it had done her the world of good. She'd laid in bed reading her book on a Sunday morning. Let her cup of tea go cold on the bedside table. Left the heating on when she went out. Had time to think. Sat in the front room late at night and turned the telly off, listened to the clock tick and the tiny voices inside her murmur. Listened closely to what they were saying.

A thunderous roar suddenly from the stadium. The crowd start singing again, full-throated, joyous. Thousands of voices lifted together in celebration. One of the kids playing near the multi-coloured gates of the primary school lifts the bottom of his shirt over his head and runs around, aeroplane arms outstretched.

Ye-e-e-e-e-e-esssss!

They follow the road round into Thoresby Street. Not far now. Louise knows she's late for the pub. Late for Kevin. She thinks about turning her phone back on to check the time, but doesn't want to see the barrage of missed calls and messages. Anyway, what does it matter? Let him wait. Won't kill him, waiting.

– Nearly there, love.

– Are we going to the house? the old lady says.

– Yeah, I'm taking you home, love. Not far now.

– Oh, I hope Maureen's in. I hope she's not gone out.

– Is Maureen your daughter?

– Eh? The old lady looks up sharply at Louise.

– Who's Maureen, love? Is it your daughter?

– Maureen? She's my neighbour. She'll have the key.

– Key?

Oh bloody hell...

– Have you lost your key, love?

No answer. She's looking down now, concentrating on walking. Each footstep is a labour. Louise can hear her wheezing, a sharp whistle under each breath. She wonders how old she is. Mid-seventies, at least. A daughter who works at Needlers. When did Needlers close down? Twenty years ago? Thirty? Louise wonders where her daughter is now. If she knows that her mam is wandering about the freezing cold streets in her slippers?

They arrive at Thoresby Terrace, finally. They stand at the top and look down the row of houses.

– Here we are, love, says Louise. – Which number is it?

The old lady looks at Louise.

– Which number does Maureen live at?

– Number nine, she says. – Maureen's number nine.

Number nine. The fifth house along. Louise takes the old lady's hand and moves it gently away from her arm. Tells her to wait there. She strides up to the front door of number nine and knocks on the door, once, twice, three times. The living room curtains are closed. Louise bends down and taps on the glass, tries to peer inside through the gap.

She comes back to where the old lady is stood.

– There's nobody in, love.

– Oh dear... oh... erm... The old lady puts her hand to her mouth. – She must have moved, she says.

– Moved? Which is your house, love? Is it number seven or number eleven?

– Oh dear, says the old lady. – Oh, I'm so sorry... oh, I am silly.

– Is there nobody else you can knock for?

– They'll have all moved away...

Louise looks at her and then she understands.

– Is this where you used to live, love?

The old lady looks away. She looks terrified, like she's about to start crying.

– Oh, I am sorry, she says.

– Don't worry, love, Louise tells her. – Don't worry, it's alright. Have you got your purse on you? Can I have a look in your pockets?

No answer. The old lady looks down the terrace at the front doors of the houses.

– I'm just going to look in your pockets, love. See if I can find anything. Alright? I'm just gonna put me hand in here...

Louise puts her hand slowly into the old lady's coat pocket and feels something small and hard. She pulls it out. A door key attached by string to a rectangle of cardboard. Written in large black capitals:

ISOBEL CASEY – 34 SALISBURY STREET, HU5.

She gets her mobile out and switches it back on.

13:45. BEEP-BEEP-BEEP-BEEP.

The screen lights up with a succession of green speech bubbles. Louise presses the HOME key and they disappear. She scrolls through her contacts for a taxi number, presses CALL, listens to the ring tone.

She looks at the old lady.

– Don't worry, Isobel, she says. – Soon have you back home and in the warm.

She orders a taxi and they tell her it's on its way.

Louise turns her phone off, puts it back in her pocket.

– Don't worry, Isobel, she says. – Won't be long.

The crowd start singing again.

Working Away

Hull... fuckin Hull lad; ever been there? No, course yer haven't, coz *you* haven't been dragged out there on graft duty by B an' their Graham, his big-shot dickhead of an uncle. Fuck up of a job that was, man, telling yer. The G man drove us both over there one Monday morning, running his head off all down the motorway. Bad jockey him, lad. Spent most of the ride lecturing us both on how to carry on, like how to conduct ourselves, yeah? As if we were going to some mad turf town.

Jesus, lad, Hull. Fuck all there, 'cept for some empty docks an' a few empty pubs an' a load of scabby no-marks sat rotting in their shit-holes, watching fuckin *X Factor*, drinking and smoking theirselves stupid coz they live in the arse end of nowhere an' there's fuck all else to do. There's hardly no shops, even. City of Culture? Is right. Don't make me fucking laugh. Ghost town more like. The bit we were in, anyway. Just a load of back to backs near a big Asda.

We had a decent gaff there, though, me an' B. Big plasma TV, boss sound system, wooden floors, big leather couch. All kitted out, like. I don't know how long their Graham had been there, but he'd obviously had enough of the local scenery. He didn't even stop for a brew, he was just like, ere y'are, there's the keys, there's the money, there's the phone. Someone would be round the next day, he said. Lad called Whoever. Then he jumped back in the motor an' did one. An' that was us lad, grafting in Hull.

It was sound at first, though. We got the connection an' set this little joey on, serving up in his flat. We never went near the place. It was all top-up jobs an' just generally keeping an eye on things. Their Graham would come over once a month with the parcel, collect the dough, an' once every so often one of us would go back home with him while the other one held the fort. It was sound. Graham had a load of regulars an' we pretty much carried on where he'd left off; the scouser on the end of the phone. Different names and faces, same accent. All the same to that load of inbreeds. There was just us, like, no opposition. No drama. Gotta hand it to G, he'd done the groundwork. Laughing, la. Or we should have been, well.

The only problem was B. Back home he was nuttin, just another contender likes, but once he landed in woolly back land he turned into friggin Al Pacino. Started giving it the big one, throwing his weight around an' terrorizing the locals. Giving it all the gangster bollocks.

One time, this joey was late coming round with the coin, only, what, half an hour or something, but B went sick on him. Not just a slap either, proper digs lad. The poor little get's eye was out *here*. No fuckin need, man. B fucked him off after that. Said he'd had a vision about it coming on top coz of this joey. B was always having visions. He'd have at least one a week. Just pure para, lad. He'd take, what, *dislikes* to people. Him, he'd go, he's a fuckin grass, him. Anyone he didn't like the look of: he's a nonce, he's a dickhead, he's a gobshite. Sit there in the pad he would, ranting and raving, throwing his blade at the door. One lad, B was convinced he was a spy sent to have us over, just coz the lad had a bit of a Manc accent. Just some little soft-arsed speccy student lid from fucking Rochdale or somewhere, but B had a vision he was working undercover for some rival firm an' ended up half choking him to death an' kicking him down a flight of stairs. Just madness, lad. No fuckin need.

Shame he didn't have no vision when it came to that tart, though. It was obvious it was all gonna go tits up from the minute he clocked her at that party. Even I could see that one coming. She was one of them - all loud and in yer face, all tits and teeth and make-up. Hate to see a gerl plastered in make-up, me. I like the natural look. B though, he was all over her and she was like oh God, I love yer accent an' all that crap and B's playing up to it, telling her his da used to know the Beatles an' Stevie Gerrard is his bezzie, all that shite. Next thing I know she's staying over at the gaff an' B's laying on bits of gear an' I'm like B what the fuck, send her round the joey's, don't bring her round here, lad. But B's like no, she's sound, she's alright, her.

I fuckin knew, though.

She had a kid, this tart, and she lived up on that newer estate. Nice houses up there. I think she'd just got divorced or got some pay off from somewhere, insurance job or sumthin, coz she always seemed to have plenty of dough. She'd have these parties at hers on a Friday or Saturday night after the boozer an' all the local talent would turn up and have it large. So B starts throwing the beak round, racking up these big poodle legs an' laying on the ozzies until eventually he's like ey gerl, just take a regular drop, square up the next month, yeah? So now she's walking off with big bags of white and brown an' she's sorting out half of the estate. Fair play though; she keeps it tight for a good while an' the orders are going up an' the dough's coming in like clockwork, B's getting his dick sucked an' the G man's happy, so everyone's a winner.

But how she fucked up was this:

I goes round for the money one Monday afternoon an' I'm tapping on the door but there's no answer. I can hear the telly going though, an' the dog's barking its head off, so I go round the back an' look through the window. I can see her zonked out on the couch, her an' her mate. I bang hard on the back door but they're not shifting. I try the handle an' it's open so I just goes in an' tries to shake her awake. They're on the nod, the pair of them, drool hanging out of their gobs, burnt foil on the arm of the couch. The place was fucking minging, lad; piles of dirty clothes everywhere and plates of half eaten scran an' it smells like the dog's pissed somewhere. She's got this scruffy little terrier thing that looks like it hasn't eaten for about three weeks. I look in the kitchen an' there's no food in its bowl so I open a tin of grub an' give it a feed. Poor little bastard nearly takes my hand off it was that starved. Eventually this tart wakes up an' she's like what, what's going on? I'm like, c'mon gerl, payday, an' she's moaning an' groaning but eventually she drags her arse off the couch an' digs out some dough, but she's half a ton short. I'm like what's this, there's fifty bar missing. It's alright, she's saying, I'll sort it tomorrow with B, no drama she says, like I'm just some lid she can fuck off. Then she climbs back under her duvet an' falls back into the land of nod.

I goes back an' tells B, I says ey, that gerl's fifty bar short an' B's like alright, alright, I'll go an sort it later. B, I says, she's a fuckin bag head, lad. I'll sort it, he says. An' lo an' behold, she turns up later that night with the dough an' B's all like, I told yer so, no need to come on top is there, she's sound. But he's acting like a twat here an' we both know it. No lay-ons to bag heads. Simple fuckin rule, lad. But she's hypnotized him with her fanny hasn't she, so he's forgetting the basics. An' once you start making exceptions that's you fucked, lad. Seen it a thousand times.

But there's no telling B, an' he even gets the nark with me for, what, doubting his judgment or something.

But I fuckin knew, lad.

Next thing is, she's round sobbing her heart out coz her ex has took the kid away. I come back from the Chinese one night with some scran an' she's there on the couch, hysterical, babbling her head off, her eyes all running black with make-up. B's going off his cake, wanting this lad's address, saying he's gonna go round an' cut the bastard's throat, an' I'm like whoa whoa, what the fuck? I get him in the kitchen on his own an' I'm like B, fuck this lad, get her out of here, none of our fuckin business, lad. But he's like a shark who's caught a whiff of blood in the water an' he's ranting on about taking fucking liberties an' you don't take a child away from his mother an' all this shite. Eventually I calm them both down an' she gets off with another big bag of brown.

Next time I goes round there's nobody there. An' the next day an' the day after that. All the doors are locked, all the curtains closed. I can hear the dog barking his head off, but there's no one at home. I said to B, what did I fuckin tell yer, she's fuckin done one, lad. He loses the head an' fuckin goes for me. We're rolling round on the floor giving each other digs. Fuckin madness, lad. He boots me in the ribs an' fucks off out to the boozer. Bad fuckin dickhead him, lad. I cleans up the gaff while he's out an' he comes back three hours later, still in a proper nark, won't talk to me. Just stands there in the kitchen, flinging his blade into the door.

Their Graham comes down the next day an' there's a big row about the money. Fuckin B's given this tart an ounce of brown an' the books aren't balancing. He says fuck all to their Graham about this, just spins him some tale about some no-mark giving us the run around. Get it fuckin sorted, says the G man, or *I'll* sort it. B's like yeah yeah yeah, no sweat, it'll be sound. I say nuttin, me. Say fuck all.

We're straight round this tart's the next day, the pair of us. On the Saturday this was, dead sunny, red hot day. There's a house full, music banging out, she's in the back garden holding court with all her little followers, about ten of 'em all sat drinking an' smoking weed. There's a paddling pool full of water an' two or three little kiddies splashing about. Laughing an' joking they all are, but this tart, her face goes deathly fuckin white when she sees me an' B. She's like hiya B, hiya T, wanna drink lads? Go on Carl, she says to this little joey, go an' get the lads a beer from the fridge. No, tell yer what, says B, *you* go an' get us a beer. Come ed, he says, an' he gets a grip of her arm and lifts her up out of this plastic chair, rough, like. This lad's like, ey, whoa, hang on a minute an' he puts his tinny down, starts getting up like, but B turns round an kicks him full in the bollocks and that's him out the game. All of a sudden, no fucker's laughing any more.

B drags this tart up an' marches her into the kitchen. She's screaming an' carrying on, tries to pull free like, but he gives her a couple of slaps round the chops an' grabs her round the chin, slams her up against the fridge.

Money, he says. She's like B, what's all this for, what you doing, why you being like this? She's terrified, lad. The dog comes skittering into the kitchen an' starts barking. The kid's there as well, this little lad about five or six. Mam, he says, Mam, Mam, an' he starts crying. Get that fucking kid out of here, shouts B, an' this gerl comes running through an' scoops the little lad up an' whisks him away. The dog's running round in circles, barking its head off. I take a step towards it, stamp hard on the floor like, an' it backs off a bit but keeps barking. Fucking thing. There's kids all wailing and carrying on in the back garden now. I'm thinking about the neighbours.

B, I say. But he's not listening, lad.

Money, he says. Fuckin money, now. He's snarling right into her face an' she's properly shat it now, she's almost fuckin collapsing with fear. I haven't got it, she says. You *wha?* shouts B, an' he bangs her head off the fridge door, once, twice. She tries to say something but it's just a kinda strangled sob like, I can't make out the words, an' B bangs her head again, harder this time, stuff falling and crashing about in the fridge, an' I'm like B, lerrer speak lad, she can't speak. So B lets go of her throat, grabs an' handful of hair an' he's like wha? *Wha?* I've not sold any, she says. I've not sold any. Please, she says. Please. Alright, says B, gis the fuckin bag back then.

I can't, she says. The dog's eaten it, she says.

The *dog?* B looks at her like she's mental. Fuck off, he says.

Swear down, she says. I hid it in a big bag of crisps and he pulled it out the cupboard. He fuckin ate it, I fuckin swear to yer.

B lets go of her an' she just crumples to the floor. She's pissed herself with fright, lad. There's a big black patch down the front of her leggings. B grabs hold of the dog an' picks it up. The dog's going mad, eyeballs pure bulging, snarling an' thrashing about, but B's got a proper grip, the head facing away from him an' it's only a little terrier, lad, just a fuckin ankle-biter.

Get that fucking lead, he says. There's a lead hanging up on the back of the door. I unhook it and follow B into the back garden.

The kids are crying in a huddle near the fence with these two girls holding them. Most of the others have done one out the back way, but there's a few heads still stood around, not knowing what the fuck to do.

B clips the lead onto the dog's collar an' throws the other end over the washing line. The dog's howling now, proper fuckin howling, lad, like a wolf; like it knows what's going down. A couple of these dickheads have got their mobies out, filming it, like. B lets go of the dog and pulls it up tight, ties it to the washing line. The fuckin thing's thrashing about an' gurgling, fucking choking, lad, its little legs going ten to the dozen.

B pulls his blade out an' I can't look, lad. I hear this kid say fuckin hell, no, an' there's screaming coming from over near the fence. I look back an' B's sliced the dog's belly clean open with his knife. It all just fell out, all the guts and what have yer, all purple and pink, just hanging down, lad. And that howl, Jesus, like the worst sound you've ever heard in your fuckin life. An' the smell, fuck me. Like fresh shit lad, no lie. Proper fuckin minging.

That's when I got off, after that. That was enough for me. I rang their Graham up an' told him I was coming home. I said to him, send your Lance or Stevie, I've had enough. Is right. Fucking Hull, la. Bad fuckin gaff. Don't ever go.

The Bell

You're fat, Debs tells him. Look at you, she says, it's hanging over your belt. Fatty Boomsticks, she says.

Simon turns side-on and looks at himself in the wardrobe mirror. I'm not that bad, he says. Fatty Boomsticks? That's a bit much. He sucks his gut in, holds it there, breathes out. He feels his stomach settle back against his belt. It feels uncomfortable. He adjusts the belt around his waist, pulls it further down so it sits on the top of his hips. He can feel the buckle digging into his flesh.

His wife is right. He *has* let himself go.

I'm forty-three, he says. It's only natural. Your metabolism slows down, he says.

Debs is sat at her dressing table in her dressing gown, applying mascara, her new clothes hung up on the wardrobe door, a top and skirt that she'd brought back from town that afternoon.

You know what you should do, she says. You should get a bike. Conrad has got a bike. A racer. He goes out with a load of others. Him and his mates. Every Sunday. They've all got bikes. They ride all over, all over the countryside. They go on the Wolds. Eighty miles he did one day, she said.

Conrad was Abi's husband. Abi was Debs' friend. They went for drinks on the last Friday of every month, Abi and

69

Debs and a few other women from the office where they worked. Tonight was one of those nights.

You're right, Simon says. I should do something about it. Get back into the gym. Get on the treadmill.

Debs pulls a face in the mirror. You won't though, she says. You say you will, but you won't.

Why won't I? he says.

You just won't. Anyway, never mind the gym, there's a park at the end of the road. You can run round that for free.

She clicks the mascara brush back into the bottle and stands up, shrugs her dressing gown to the floor. She is in her underwear, matching purple bra and knickers. They look new. Simon tries to remember if he has seen them on her before. She turns away from the mirror and unhooks her new top from the wardrobe door. Catches him staring at her.

What you looking at? she says.

Nothing, says Simon, and turns away. He busies himself picking stray socks and dirty T-shirts off the floor, sniffs them and dumps them into the laundry basket.

Where you off, anyway? he says.

I told you, just round Old Town, she says.

*

He's in the front room watching TV when she comes downstairs. She looks immaculate, like she has stepped from the front cover of a glossy magazine. She gathers up her handbag, phone and keys from the coffee table.

What time do you reckon you'll be back? he asks.

Don't know, she says. Not late.

She leans down and pecks him lightly on the cheek. He can smell her scent, heavy and sweet. It is almost as if she is saturated in perfume. It clings to her hair and her clothes.

Have a nice time, he says.

I will, she says.

*

Simon heats up a Tesco lasagne in the microwave. He eats half of it out of the plastic tray and then leaves the rest on the kitchen table. He goes back upstairs, closes the curtains, puts on the bedside light and takes off his shirt and jeans and socks. He stands in front of the mirror in his boxer shorts. His belly sags. His man-tits sag. He sucks his gut in and flexes a circus strongman pose, fists clenched, biceps hard. They're still there. Forty-three-years-old. He turns around slowly, looking at himself in the mirror. Tries to imagine what his body will look like in twenty years' time; ten, even.

He gets down on the floor and lies flat on his back. He clasps his hands behind his head and pulls himself upright. It is harder than he thought it would be. He lifts his legs and tries again, tries to touch his knees with his forehead. It feels a little easier, but not much. He can feel the folds of flab concertina around his midriff. He manages fourteen sit-ups before he feels out of breath. He lays back down flat for a while. There is a dull ache in the small of his back and a thin film of sweat on his chest. He lies there and listens to his own breathing. He can see a thick spider web in the corner of the ceiling near the wardrobe. He stares at it for a while before rolling over and pushing himself up from the floor. He sprays Lynx

Africa under his arms and around his torso before getting dressed again and going downstairs to the living room.

He watches TV and drinks cans of John Smiths Bitter. He watches *Britain's Got Talent*, then turns over to a documentary about polar bears in the Antarctic. Then he watches an old *Top of The Pops* from 1982. That dark haired one out of Bananarama, he used to fancy her back in the day. He wonders what she looks like now. He considers going upstairs to the laptop, but he can't be bothered to move. Besides, Debs will be back soon. Simon thinks about how the human body will always move towards pleasure and avoid pain. Instinct, he thinks. Survival technique. Or laziness. He can't decide. He decides to stop thinking about it. He works his way through five cans of beer and jumps between TV channels. Cops chasing kids around motorways and housing estates, canned laughter on American sit-coms, panel shows and football.

He falls asleep on the settee just after 1 a.m. and does not hear her key turn the lock or her fumbling as she removes her shoes in the hallway, her stocking feet tiptoeing past the living room door and up the stairs to bed.

*

Seven a.m., and Simon is on his second lap of the park, Underworld banging in his earphones. He runs clockwise around the central green, past the big houses, past the flats, past the Victorian Conservatory and the playground. His calf muscles are starting to tighten and he can feel a dampness spreading across his chest. He concentrates on his breathing and tries to syncopate his footfall to the hard beats being piped into his head. As he nears the ice-cream hut, he sees a figure on the road coming the other way, another runner, a large young lad in grey jogging bottoms and sweat shirt. He's at least six-and-a-half feet tall and hugely heavy. He lurches forward with each step, like a dray horse hit by a tranquilizer dart. As they pass each other, the lad gives Simon a brief gasping nod of acknowledgement. His face is puffy and crimson. He looks like he's about to have a heart attack. Simon looks at him then looks quickly away, keeps his eyes fixed on concrete for the next two long and torturous laps.

*

The shop is cramped and smells of oil and rubber and the bikes are hung from the ceiling in rows on either side. The man is small and wiry. He wears a tight dark blue top zipped to the throat and shiny black shorts that look as though they've been sprayed onto his legs. His calf muscles stand out like slabs of rock. He stands on his tiptoes, as if permanently primed for fight or flight. He is very helpful. He points out the different models and goes through their capabilities and limitations. He explains the gear systems and wheel types and the different types of terrains they are each suited to. Simon is impressed with his knowledge.

I never knew there was so much to it, he told the man. I thought a bike was just a bike, he said. The man laughed. You can get a bit obsessed about it all, said the man. It can get like an illness. I just want a standard one, says Simon. A beginner's bike. Nothing too ambitious. Do you want to do road work? asks the man. I don't want to do any kind of work, says Simon. Just something to trundle about on. Go to work on it, a few laps of the park, maybe.

The man tugs at his beard, thinks about this, then points out a dark green machine above their heads. He fetches a small step-ladder and climbs up level with the bike, unhooks it from the fastening and passes it down. It is heavier than Simon expected. The way the man handled it with one hand, Simon had expected it to be as light as anything, but the weight of it surprises him and he has to quickly use both hands to stop the bike from dropping. Even so, the tyres bounce on the floor and the bell sounds a *ding!* The man steps down from the ladder and holds the bike by the handlebars, invites Simon to sit upon it. Try that for size, he says. That's a twenty inch.

It's an old-fashioned sit-up-and-beg type of affair. British racing green. Full mudguards. Brown leather saddle and brown handlebar grips. The sort of bike a grocer from the 1950s would ride, thinks Simon. He hitches up his jeans and swings his leg over. He balances himself on the saddle and holds the handlebars. They seem wider apart than he expected. His toes barely touch the floor on either side and for one brief second he panics, thinks he is going to lose his balance and tumble over, send all the other machines crashing. He lets go with one hand and grabs the man's shoulder, one foot on the floor.

Whoa, he says. He laughs. Nearly went there. I haven't ridden a bike since I was at school, he says. Not since I had a paper round. You're OK, says the man, it's the right size. You won't fall.

Simon takes his hand off the man's shoulder and grabs the handlebar, shifts his weight from side to side, his toes pushing off the floor: left, right, left, right. That's fine, says the man, watching him. You could maybe even do to have that seat raised a touch. Raised? says Simon. I don't want it any higher, surely? I'll fall off! You won't fall off, the man tells him. You'll be fine.

Simon spins one of the pedals backwards with the top of his foot and stops it there, his other foot planted on the floor. He sits up straight in the saddle and imagines looking out over a waving field of corn from the side of a country lane on a warm summer's day.

How does it feel? asks the man.

It feels great, says Simon.

*

Debs comes back from town the next day with a pair of padded black cycling shorts and a fluorescent yellow top. You'll need some proper road shades as well, she tells him. Oakley do a nice pair. Do you want Conrad's number? No, you're alright, he tells her. Simon likes Abi, but he has never really got on with her husband. Too loud and brash and self-confident, all hearty man-hugs and assumed familiarity. Once, the four of them had gone out for a curry and Simon had watched appalled as Conrad casually smashed the stack of poppadums with his fist and doled out the fragments onto everyone's plate whilst extolling the virtues of Nigel Farage at an uncomfortable volume. He laughed uproariously at his own crude and obvious jokes. He beckoned waiters with a raised digit. Simon had spent the meal in a near mute state of subdued detachment, which prompted narrowed eyebrows and kicks under the table from Debs. They had driven home in icy silence that night and Simon had declined all future group engagements.

I want to go out on my own at first, Simon tells her. Get used to it.

Put the gear on, she says.

It's not that sort of bike, he says.

*

He pedals along the back roads, moving steadily up through the gears. He squeezes the brakes well in advance of junctions and slows down for approaching vehicles. After a while he gains confidence, leaning into corners and swaying in and out between parked cars. The wind pushes his hair back and flaps at his jacket. He nods at passing cyclists on the other side of the road. Simon feels a rush of mild exhilaration. He turns onto the main avenue and it's empty, no traffic around, so he stands on the pedals, cranking up the pace, and he doesn't see the speed bump. Both wheels leave the road and thump back down.

Ding!

The bell smites a single note, high and bright and true, and Simon wobbles momentarily but his natural speed corrects him and he holds his nerve and steadies himself. He rides around the Avenues until dusk begins to fall and he remembers he hasn't got any lights. He returns home and locks the bike up in the back room.

*

The next day is a Monday and it is warm, the streets bathed in bright sunshine by 7 a.m. Simon decides to ride the bike to work. He finds an old rucksack in the back of the wardrobe and puts his packed lunch inside, straps it to his back and sets off.

Halfway down Princes Avenue, he becomes aware of a noise coming from the bike. It's the bell. Every slight dip or dink in the tarmac elicits a faint jangling. Simon pulls over to the pavement and dismounts. He unscrews the top of the bell and gazes blankly at the workings beneath; a white plastic arm with two discs of metal at either end atop a small cog. He lifts the arm free of the casing and flicks the bell lever so it spins the cog around. He puts his ear down to the handlebars and gives it another spin, listens. Silence. Simon replaces the arm and tightens the casing and sets off again. But it's still there, the noise. If anything, it's more insistent, a loose metallic rattling with every turn of the pedal.

Ding... ding... ding...

Simon keeps himself focused on the road ahead. Tries to tune it out.

When he arrives at work his shirt is damp and stuck to his spine. He locks up the bike in the foyer and ducks into the men's toilets, unbuttons his shirt and rubs paper towels beneath his arms. He splashes his face and neck with cold water then turns the hand dryer nozzle upwards and leans over the hot blast of air.

*

He works through his lunch break and leaves an hour early. The bell rattles and tinkles with every dip and bump on the road, with every turn of the wheels. Simon grits his teeth through the traffic and heads for Princes Avenue.

The shop is still open. The man is sat behind the counter watching something on his phone. He looks up as Simon wheels the bike through the door.

Alright? he says

Yes, hello, says Simon. I'm afraid there's a bit of a problem.

The man puts his phone down and comes from behind the counter.

What's up?

Simon lifts the bike and bounces it off the floor, once, twice.

Can you hear that? he says.

The man squats down on his haunches and surveys the chain and the gear cogs.

What am I listening for? he asks.

That, says Simon. He rocks the bike from side to side. The bell jangles. The man shakes his head, looks up at Simon.

What?

Can't you hear it?

Do you mean the bell?

Yeah!

The man straightens up and puts his hand on the bell, thumbs the lever. It sounds with a sweet silver *ding!*

What's up with it? he says.

It just constantly rattles, says Simon. When you ride it, I mean. Jingle jangle, jingle jangle. All the time.

The man looks at Simon.

Well, it will do, he says.

What do you mean it will do? It's supposed to do that, is it?

The man shrugs.

It's a two hundred pound bike, mate, he says. You get what you pay for.

So I'm supposed to just put up with that, am I? That constant rattling and ding-ding-dinging?

Well, take it off then, says the man.

What, the bell?

Yeah.

Simon considers this for a moment.

And what if I want to warn someone out the way?

The man smiles.

Shout at 'em, he says.

Simon bites his lip. He feels hot and uncomfortable. The late afternoon sun beats through the full-length windows and glints off the suspended bicycles; red bicycles, yellow bicycles, black and green and blue and brilliant white. Banks of shiny metal suspended above his head. Simon thinks that he can smell himself, the sweat seeping from beneath his arms.

I'm not happy, he says.

*

That night Simon has a dream. He is trying to run away from someone or something demonic, an unseen predator snarling and snorting and snapping its teeth just behind him. He is trying to get away but he is enormously fat, a huge bloated Sumo-sized man with inflated thighs and a massive swaying belly. He is so fat he can hardly move. He tries to run, but it is like trying to haul himself through treacle. He can feel his heart hammering, as though it is about to burst from his chest. His feet are turning, pounding the ground beneath him, but he is hardly moving. He can almost feel the heat from the beast's slavering mouth at the back of his neck.

He awakes with a start. The curtains are drawn back and the room is warm with sunlight. Simon takes a few moments to compose himself and shake the dream from his head. Then he showers, gets dressed and follows the smell of freshly brewed coffee down to the kitchen where Debs is sat in her dressing gown, reading a magazine. Simon glances at the clock. Seven thirty-five.

Not working today? he asks her.

Nope. Off to York with Abi, she says, not looking up.

Why didn't you wake me? he says. I'll be late.

He opens and closes drawers, fishes in the pockets of jackets hung in the hallway.

What you looking for? asks Debs.

Car keys, he says.

I thought you were going in on your bike, she says. Every day, you said?

I'm going to be late, he says.

You'll be a lot quicker on the bike, she says. Traffic's stood still at this time.

He doesn't answer, keeps rooting around in various places. Opens every drawer, slams objects around on the worktops. Lifts a bunch of bananas from the fruit bowl.

Simon, she says.

OH FOR THE LOVE OF CHRIST! he shouts.

He stomps out of the back door and returns minutes later, pushing his bike by the handlebars. He hauls it through the kitchen and down the hallway, the bell ding-dinging as the wheels bounce off the skirting boards.

FUCKS SAKE SIMON! she yells, but the front door slams and he's gone.

*

He stops at Sainsbury's on the way into work and buys a can of deodorant. He locks himself in a toilet booth at work and takes off his shirt, sprays himself all over. He sits at his desk and taps quietly away at his computer, processing figures and firing off reports on email, barely exchanging a word with his colleagues. At half past eleven he gets up and goes to the gents' toilet where he locks himself in a booth and plays Solitaire on his phone. Then he clicks onto a mobile porn site, turns the sound down and watches a video of a blonde woman having sex with two heavily tattooed men. He massages himself through his trousers, but his body is not responding. He turns off his phone and stays in the booth until his legs begin to go dead. Then he washes his hands and splashes water on his face and goes back into office, stands at his supervisor's desk. She looks up from her screen, her smile dissolving when she sees the look on his face.

Now then, Simon, she says. What's up?

I need to go home, he says. I feel sick.

OK, she says. She looks at him doubtfully. You do look a bit off-colour. Have you eaten something?

I just feel sick, he says. And I've got a headache. My head is pounding. He closes his eyes, kneads his temples with his fingers.

Well, OK, get yourself to doctors, she says.

Thank you, he says.

*

The bell jingles almost constantly as Simon pedals through the city centre. He tries to silence it by cupping it with one hand, but he cannot steer properly and almost wobbles off when a heavy lorry passes him. When he reaches Princes Avenue, he stops and dismounts. He leans the bike up against the railings outside the delicatessen and crosses the road over to the bars and cafes. The first few lunchtime punters are sat at the tables outside. Simon walks into Garbutts and orders a pint of Stella, takes it outside. He sits and drinks and watches the people walk past. The bike is still there, where he left it. He drains the pint and goes back inside for another, plus a whisky chaser. The day's newspapers are stacked up by the side of the bar. Simon bangs down the whisky, selects *The Guardian* and returns to his seat outside. He reads an article on Brexit and sips at his lager, more slowly this time. Occasionally, he glances up and looks at his bike. It is still there. Simon can feel the alcohol begin to work. His head starts to swim and he finds it hard to concentrate on the words. Eventually, he folds the paper away and just sits there, watching.

A young lad walks past the bike, stops and looks at it. He scopes his surroundings for a few seconds then squats down as if tying his shoelace. Then he straightens up again and takes the bike by the handlebars, swings his leg over and pedals off slowly, more slowly than Simon expected. Simon watches him disappear down Clumber Street then finishes off his pint and rises from the table.

There's a group of men and women sat outside Westbourne House. Some of them have cans in their hands. Simon stops and digs into his pocket, pulls out a ten pound note, hands it to one of the men.

Here you go, he says. Have a drink on me.

Fuckin hell, nice one bro, says the man.

My pleasure, says Simon.

It's quiet on the Avenues. The heat hums heavy in the early afternoon and the sunshine dapples the road. Simon crosses over from the shadows cast by the tall houses and walks on the sunny side of the street. He starts to sing a song to himself: *It's a lovely day for saying it's a lovely day...* He wonders where he's heard the tune before. He starts to laugh to himself.

Pissed, he thinks. Pissed on a school day.

When he gets home the mortice key is not locked and the alarm isn't on. The house feels cool and strangely quiet. He goes through to the kitchen and starts assembling bread, butter, cheese and mayonnaise from the fridge. A sandwich, he thinks. A big fuck off double decker sandwich. And some crisps. Fuck it. He starts rooting about in the cupboards, slamming doors.

He doesn't notice Debs until she says his name. She stands in the kitchen doorway. She looks flustered, her face and neck flushed pink as though she has been exercising.

Oh, hiya Debs, he says. Have we got any crisps?

What are you doing home? she says, but she doesn't sound angry or accusatory. Simon was expecting the Spanish Inquisition, but Debs seems concerned, anxious almost.

He is about to reply when he senses a movement in the hallway behind her. He steps back from the worktop, looks beyond her and sees the face of a man he struggles to place for a second. Then he realizes who it is.

Conrad! he says. How are you, mate?

Conrad advances down the hallway and hovers at Debs' shoulder. He smiles, nods.

Simon, he says. Good thanks.

Conrad is giving me and Abi a lift to York, says Debs.

Course he is, says Simon. Is he taking you on his fucking bike?

Neither of them say anything. They just stand there and look at him. Simon laughs and opens a drawer, takes out a kitchen knife.

Simon, says Debs, are you OK?

I've never felt better in my life, he says.

Go To A Grown-Up

Let's say this happens on a busy dual-carriageway near a secondary school on a sweltering day in June, around half past four in the afternoon. You're on your way to the garage for something to wake you up – an energy drink or a bar of chocolate, something like that. You're due on the evening shift and have not long woken up. The day has been hot, the air thick and you're still a little punch-drunk with the remnants of that deep afternoon sleep. You yawn and scratch your belly and amble along, enjoying the heat, glad to be out of that stupid costume and in your normal clothes. There are not that many of your fellow citizens around. Most of the kids from the school have gone home, just a few stragglers in blue and yellow uniforms passing you in ones and twos. Everything seems bright and vivid after the curtained gloom of your room. There are no clouds in the sky and the sun is bouncing off the pavements and windows. There's a bad taste in your mouth. Should have brushed your teeth before you came out. You have slept too heavily and need to wake up. Two energy drinks. A shower and a change of shirt when you get back. Busy night ahead of you.

You don't notice the cars slowing down on the opposite side of the road as the lights turn to amber and you don't see the girl running through the two lines of traffic until she's right there in front of you. She's holding something out to you. You don't understand what is going on. What is it that she wants? She's trying to give you something. A phone. She wants you to take her phone. She's small and looks young, no more than eleven or twelve. The fear in her face makes her look even younger.

– Can you talk to my Dad for me? she says.

– Your dad? you say to her.

– He said I should go to a grown-up, she says.

You look around. There are no other grown-up citizens nearby, not on this side of the street, anyway. There's a woman emptying orange and white carrier bags from the boot of her car, but she's a fair distance away. There's no one else. It's down to you. You are the only grown-up. But you don't feel much like a grown-up. Grown-ups are supposed to take charge of things. Take control. Most of the time, though, you feel like life is something that comes at you without warning. Like this, now. You don't know what to do. What to say. Your first impulse is to blank her, to not get involved, just keep walking. But your Spider-Sense is tingling; you can feel the panic coming off her in waves. Her face, tilted up to you, pale and pinched and anxious.

You stop and take the phone, put it to your ear.

– ... *there? Yes? Hello? Hello?* A man's voice, urgent.

– Hello, you say. – Who is this?

– *Is Lucy there?*

– Lucy? Is this your daughter?

– *Is she there?* the voice says. – *Is she with you?*

– She's here, you say.

– OK, I need you to listen to me, says the voice. *– There's a man bothering my daughter. Do you see him? Little fat cunt, beard. Is he there?*

You look around the street and yes, there is a man; a stocky man with a full beard in baggy knee-length shorts and a white sports vest. He's jogging along on the other side of the road. He's looking across. He's spotted the girl and yourself. He's checking the cars, waiting for a gap in the traffic.

– I can see him, you say.

– OK, now listen, says the voice, *– listen to me. He's going to try and take Lucy away. Do not let him take her away. OK?*

You start to speak. You start to say something, but the voice cuts you off:

– I'm on my way now. OK? I'M COMING NOW. DO NOT LET HIM TAKE HER. OK?

And before you can offer another word, the phone is dead in your hand and the man with the beard is through the cars and running across the road. And then he's there and the girl has darted behind you. She takes a tight hold on the back of your shirt.

– Come on Lucy, he says. – Stop being silly. He steps around you, goes to grab hold of her and she dodges his grasp, pulls you around to face him again.

– Lucy, says the man.

– Get away from me, she says.

– Bro, you say, – bro, she don't wanna go with you.

– You keep out of it, he says. – I'm her dad.

– I don't think so, you say.

The man makes another grab and the girl screams and the scream sends a pure jolt of panic through you and you push him away, but he's wide and solid; it's like trying to push a wall and he lunges right back at you and you lower your head, feel his nose bone crack against your skull and then he's hunched over, clutching at his face. The drops of red falling through his fingers and spot-spot-spotting the pavement.

The girl starts crying. You stare at this man and the blood on the pavement and you cannot believe what has happened. You reach a hand down to him, saying, – Hey, brother, I'm sorry, alright? Listen, you say, – I do not want to fight with you, my brother. Please.

He looks at his hands cupped with blood and looks at the blood on the floor and he bellows like a wounded bear and launches himself straight at you and you are knocked flying. The both of you fall hard on the floor. He is on top of you. You have your hands around his throat. His fists are wrapped around your wrists. His bristles and his hot breath on you. You can feel his teeth snapping against your cheek and your ear. He is trying to prise your wrists apart and bite at your face. He is a powerful man and he has the rage of a wild animal. It is taking all of your strength to hold him away. The girl is shrieking somewhere above you both, hysterical. He is trying to drive his knee into your groin. You lift your legs and wrap them around his waist, try to flip him over, but he is too strong, too determined. You hear a car horn sound long and loud, repeated, people shouting, and then a sharp tug of pain below your eye and the weight of the man is suddenly lifted.

And then there are hands upon you, dragging you up to your feet. You pull yourself away and turn and walk off. What the actual hell, man! What the hell. There are raised voices and shouting behind you, but you don't look back, you keep going. You can feel a wetness trickling down your cheek. Your entire face is throbbing. You wipe your cheek with your hand and look. It's red. Blood on your hand. You keep walking, fast, keep walking until the shouting is far away behind you. You pass the garage on the corner and it's then that you notice that the girl is there, right beside you, running almost, trying to keep up. She is sobbing.

– Are you OK? you say to her.

She nods yes, but cannot speak. She is breathless with shock. The two of you walk quickly together. Your heart is thumping hard and the adrenaline is banging around your blood. You feel electric, like you have been plugged into something.

– Is he following us? you say.

She says, – I don't know, I don't know.

You look behind you, but there is nobody.

You cannot believe what has just occurred back there. It is almost like a dream. Your mouth is as dry as stone and you can feel a hard knot forming on the back of your head. You feel dizzy and sick and your breath is coming hard. The day is swimming in and out of focus. You need to calm down, stop, get some water. You go into the garage and the girl follows you.

It is cool in there. Piped-in pop music. It is like nothing bad has happened. The refrigerated shelves of milk and juice and water. You open a door and pull out two bottles. Your shirt, stuck to your stomach with sweat, feels cold. The woman behind the till stares at your face. You pay for the water and some paper napkins and leave.

The pair of you step back outside. There are people around, but none of them are looking at you. You give the girl a bottle of water and you head back to your street. You take the long way round, up the long snaking road that cuts across the back of the school and leads through to the ten-foots. You go past back gardens full of washing lines and barbed-wire topped fences. You can hear people sat talking, music and TVs playing through open windows and doors. You feel like there are a million pairs of eyes peering out from behind back-bedroom curtains. The girl has her phone up at her ear. She is trying to talk slowly and carefully, trying to catch her breath, but has started crying again. She is saying something about Darren, about her Mam and this Darren. This must be the beard man, you think.

– Why can't I just live with you, Dad? she's saying.

You try not to listen. You do not want to be involved. You dab at your face with a handful of napkins. There is a lot of blood. You use up nearly all of the packet. One side of your face feels as though it is on fire and your eye is starting to close. It feels swollen. This is not good. You have to get home. You have a medicine cabinet at home. You need to look in the mirror. The girl is offering you the phone again. You do not want to talk to anyone. You do not want any more of this. But she is holding out the phone. You know what she is thinking. The beard man, he might come back. You take the phone.

– *Lucy,* says the man's voice. – *Lucy?* His voice sounds distant, like he's on hands-free. You can hear a faint noise in the background. Sounds like he's driving.

– This is Mohammed, you say.

– *What's happened? Where are you now? Are you still on Bricknell?*

– I'm going home now, you tell him. – Please, my friend, I cannot do anything more.

– *I'm almost there,* he says. – *I need you to...*

90

Then his voice disappears. You look at the screen – blank.

You hand the phone back to the girl. – Your phone has died, you tell her.

You come out of the back ten-foots and you turn left into your street. The girl follows you down to the house and stands behind you as you get your key into the door. She has stopped crying.

– I am going home now, you tell her. She doesn't say anything, just stands there looking at you. Her face is smeared wet with dirt and her eyes are large with fear.

– You must go to your parents, you tell her. – You must go now. You go. OK? Bye bye.

– What if he comes back, though? she says.

There is a siren in the distance. A police car or an ambulance, you cannot tell the difference. They are all the same. You are wet through with sweat. You can smell yourself. You need to fix up your face and have a shower. You do not want this little girl in the house, but what can you do? You cannot let her walk the streets on her own. The streets are too dangerous. There are men with beards who try to snatch children and bite your face.

– Come in, you say to her. – You can ring your father from my phone.

It is quiet in the house. It is good to be inside, to get out of the heat. You can smell food. You are hoping Nebas or Hajha will be home, but nobody answers your yells. You tell the girl to sit down in the front room and you go up to the bathroom.

You feel sick when you look in the mirror. There is an ugly purple crescent across your cheekbone. The blood is starting to scab and you can see the wet pink flesh open up when you move your jaw. You run the taps and try to clean your face as best you can with a cloth. The water in the sink is swirling red and it hurts like a thousand bee stings. You dab cautiously at the wound. You do not want to open it up any more. This will need stitches. You cannot afford to go to the hospital. If you go to the hospital you will lose your shift. You have to wait an eternity in that place. You find some gauze and cotton wool and some sticking plaster in the cabinet. You pat your face dry and patch the wound up as best as you can. You look at yourself in the mirror. You look bizarre. A big white bump on the side of your face. You look like a crazy man back from the war.

When you go back downstairs the girl is stood in the middle of the room, her bag still over her shoulder. She looks at you like she is helpless, like she doesn't know what to do. You find your phone in your jacket, which is hung up on the back of the door. You hand it to her.

– Here, you say, – call your father. He will be worried. Tell him you are safe.

But she doesn't take the phone from you. Just looks at you with helpless eyes.

– I don't know the number, she says.

Oh, dear Lord. How did this happen?

– Sit down, you say to her, – sit down.

She looks around herself, looks at the sofa. Your costume is on the sofa, a red and blue puddle. You gather it up and throw it onto the armchair so she can sit down.

She sits down, her bag clutched to herself.

– So, you say to her. – Who was that man?

– Darren, she says. – He's my Mam's boyfriend. He's horrible.

– I am thinking that we need to call the police, you say to her. – I am thinking that would be the best thing. This does not look good for me. I cannot have any trouble, you tell her.

She picks up the mask from the arm of the sofa. She holds it up, looks at it. Looks at you.

– Is this yours?

– Yes, you say.

– Why have you got a Spiderman mask?

– Because I am Spiderman, you say, and you smile at her, to let her know that this is a joke, that you are joking with her. You do not want her to be afraid.

– No you're not, she says.

– Yes, I really am, you tell her. – I am the Spiderman. This is my secret identity.

She shakes her head. She looks so serious.

– With the sign held up, you say to her. You hold your hands up as though you are holding a sign.

She must have seen you. There are a few of you around the city. There are many take-aways, many pizza shops. You stand with the signs on the side of the road. Special offers. A family of four, bargain buckets, free garlic bread. Meal deal. The children wave to you from the cars.

– I am Spiderman with the pizzas, you tell her. – For the pizza shop. You know?

She shrugs and falls silent, stares at the floor. She starts chewing on her nails. She is anxious. It has been a stressful thing for her. For both of you.

– OK, you say to her, – I am going to make some tea. Do you want some tea?

She shakes her head.

– Or a drink of water? Do you need more water? It is hot, yes?

She holds up her empty bottle, nods yes.

You go through to the back kitchen and switch the kettle on. You're getting a glass from the cupboard when you sense a movement out of the window. Something in the back garden. Your nerves are still jangling and you are startled. The glass slides from your hand and smashes on the floor. You pick up the cricket bat by the back door, stand to one side of the window and peer out. Two uniforms coming through the gate. A man and a woman. White shirt sleeves and black vests. The woman is speaking into a radio.

A bang-bang-banging on the front door.

You stand with your back to the wall, the cricket bat raised and gripped in both of your hands, ready.

The girl appears in the doorway.

– There's someone at the door, she says, panicked.

She's coming over to you. Your Spider-Sense is tingling.

– Stop there, you tell her. – Don't come near me. Just stay where you are, you say.

This is how it happened. You remember every detail.

Bohemia

They'd met at the Welly. She was wearing dungarees and had been dancing hard to drum 'n' bass. Her pale blue hair was tied back from her face and slicked with sweat. Mermaid hair. Years later, he would describe seeing her that night as some kind of vision, as if she had just walked out of the sea. She caught him smiling at her at the bar, this townie looking lad. He leant in to her beneath the noise and asked her if she'd been out grafting.

– I'm sorry, she said. I beg your pardon?

He pointed at her dungarees. – They're shoplifting pants, them, he said, and Lauren had laughed.

He wouldn't have normally said anything like that, especially not to someone like her. Nathan was usually nervous around girls, especially attractive emo-looking students from down south with well-rounded vowels and mermaid hair that smelt of apples, but on that particular night he had taken a pellet of mescaline and it lent him a calm, detached confidence; a faint bemusement, almost. His manner intrigued her. She was used to lads being lairy in bars, especially lads from Hull in polo shirts who clutched bottles of lager and slid their eyes up and down her. But this didn't feel like that. She liked this lad's eyes. They joined in when he smiled. She could see there was a softness there. They got to talking. They forgot about the friends they'd come with and retreated to a low table in a dark corner, away from the pounding of the dancefloor and the babble of the bar.

She was in the last year of Uni, a Chemistry degree. She said she liked Hull, liked the fact that it was cheap and friendly and near the sea. She said she liked the accent, too – *err nerr*, *farv ter narn* and all that. She didn't know very many locals, though. She usually came to the Welly on a Friday, but spent most of her time on campus. She said the workload got totally brutal in the last year. She asked him what he did and he told her he was a penguin trainer at the Deep and she said what, really? and he said no, not really, I work at a call-centre. He told her about some of the other jobs he'd had and how he was supposed to have had trials for City when he was fourteen but got glandular fever and was laid up for weeks. He asked her what she wanted to do when she got her degree and she said she wasn't sure, maybe something to do with textiles. She liked to make her own clothes. Yes, she had made the dungarees. No, she didn't go shoplifting.

They talked about their favourite films (*Reservoir Dogs, The Unbearable Lightness of Being, Scarface, La Dolce Vita*) music (Bruce Springsteen, Hot Chip, Stereophonics, London Grammar) and books (Franz Kafka, crime novels, Naomi Klein, footballers' biographies) and what it was like in her home town of Gloucester (boring, like, full of sheep) and then they talked about the countryside and cities of culture and spaceships and deserts and Disneyland and a thousand other things and then, for some reason, in the middle of it all, Nathan just got up and said OK, cheers, nice to meet you Lauren, look after yourself and he left.

It was nerves, he'd say later. He didn't think he had a

hope in hell of actually going home with her. But really it was because of the mescaline. He couldn't stop looking at her hair, the way it shone blue-green under the spotlights, and he had become suddenly paranoid that he was staring at her. That he was making her feel uncomfortable. So he got up and walked out of the club and wandered around down by the pier and the Marina for a bit, watched the boats bobbing in the darkness and thought about the sea and mermaids before heading home to listen to music and chain-smoke until dawn.

*

He saw her again a couple of weeks later as he was leaving a bar down Newland Avenue with some of his five-a-side mates. She ran out into the street after him and called his name. I didn't think you would remember me, he said. I can't believe you just walked away like that, she said. We need to go out again, she said. We didn't finish our conversation.

So they went out again and ended up seeing each other regularly, every week, then every two days or so and then every day and night, and after about six months they moved in together, a two-up two-down terraced house round the back of Beverley Road for seventy-five pounds a week rent. No furniture, no central heating, one gas fire in the front room and a yard full of barking Alsatians next door. It was in some state, this house. The kitchen looked like it hadn't been touched since the 1970s, all dark wood effect wall units, Formica worktops and bright orange geometric patterned wallpaper.

– Who the fuck lived here, said Nathan, – Fleetwood Mac?

– I like it, said Lauren.

*

They had a good clear year of curling up together like proper soul mates. Nathan harassed strangers on the telephone about their utility bills by day and played football on a Monday night. Lauren got up late, attended her lectures in the afternoon and worked the odd night in the University bar. Most evenings were spent drinking wine, smoking weed and watching Netflix on the laptop. Some nights they switched off all the screens and Nathan would strum his acoustic guitar while Lauren stewed over books on Organometallics. They'd slide into the bars down Newland or Princes Avenue once or twice during the week when money allowed and go clubbing at the weekend. Lauren ran up tops and dresses on a big black and silver sewing machine that she'd salvaged from a yard near Witham. She taught Nathan how to cook, big pots of vegetarian chilli and stews that kept them warm throughout the winter and damp early spring. She talked about growing their own vegetables. You can get an allotment round the back of Newland for a pound a week, she told him. Boho, he called her. Hippy Chick. Chav-tastic, she called him. Working Class Hero. Caveman.

*

That summer, Lauren graduated from University and got a job at Smith and Nephew in the labs. Good money. She took her first job very seriously and started dressing in accordance: smart skirts and tops from Zara and M&S. Plain colours, straight lines. She stopped smoking weed on a weeknight, said it made her lose her focus during the day. She chopped her hair to a chin length bob and reverted to her natural dark blonde. The sewing machine was put away on top of the wardrobe. Instead of shopping together at Lidl, they got deliveries from Sainsbury's.

– What the fuck are these? Nathan asked, holding up a small packet. – Sunflower seeds? We haven't even got a garden.

– You eat them, dickhead, she said.

– Yes, I do know, he said. – It was a joke.

Then Nathan started losing hours at the call centre. Some weeks, he'd be lucky to get two days' work. He applied for other jobs, but it was difficult. There wasn't much around. He began to slip into a state of inertia. He stayed up late drinking and smoking himself stupid, playing his Springsteen CDs loud on a week night when Lauren had to get up for work. She'd come down to a tip in the morning and it would still be a tip when she got in from work; Nathan stretched out on the couch, stoned, staring at Judge Judy surrounded by dirty plates and half-full mugs of coffee gone cold. It was like their roles had suddenly flipped, she said; he was the student and she was the worker. On a weekend, she went out with her new mates from work and Nathan stayed in.

As the months went by and their new roles became routine, they each began to form fresh opinions of the other. She said he was irresponsible and lazy. He thought she was uptight and selfish. The bickering turned to full-blown arguments that flared up closer and closer together, like lightning bolts coming in quick succession, until one Sunday afternoon the storm broke directly overhead. They had a huge fight over an unpaid gas bill that resulted in Nathan kicking a bedroom door off its hinges and storming out. After two nights on a mate's couch he came back and they tentatively made up.

But the rot had set in. Nathan and Lauren settled into a long and tedious state of mutual antagonism, not so much a break-up as a slow and painful hacking apart. All the differences that had amused and intrigued them now became points of sore contention.

Do you have to make that noise when you eat?

Can you not put that away after you?

I'll buy what I want. I'm the one who brings the money into this house.

Fucking pretentious twat.

Lazy fucking bone-idle bastard.

They were poison to each other by then and they both knew it, but still they drifted through the days and weeks, stuck together out of habit, or fear of change, or some strange subdued spite, or maybe all three.

There were things in his name and things in her name. Deposits and contracts. It seemed like less bother to just coast along in a state of subdued resentment than try and unravel it all for good.

After a while, it became almost normal.

*

Prague was supposed to be kill or cure. It was Nathan's idea. Despite the constant sniping and petty point-scoring, he still harboured faint hopes of saving the relationship. He knew he needed to do something to rejuvenate himself, to boost his self-esteem and, in turn, hopefully remind Lauren of how things used to be. He was hoping that a few days out of their usual environment would make them stop and take stock, take another good look at each other. Just the two of them. Maybe it would be enough to bring them back together. He thought Prague would be a good place to go, a place that symbolized everything Lauren loved before she discovered loyalty cards and overtime and sensible skirts. Prague meant Kafka and absinthe, Art Nouveau and black-and-white films with subtitles. She agreed to one last attempt. She took the week off work and he booked the flights.

They stayed in a pension owned by a college; bare and basic rooms vacated by students for the summer. The place was full of back-packers, new-age drifters and cut-price tourists. They had drunken desperate sex on the first night followed by a blazing argument the day after, some perceived slight or long-forgotten grievance brought lurching back to life. Accusation and counter-accusation. The next four days and nights were spent in a sullen truce. Early morning cigarettes smoked in silence save for weary exhalations and the clinking of coffee cups. Listless rounds of sightseeing, staring dumbly at statues and palaces and paintings, then later sat in some bar, chosen with a shrug, picking at meals that neither of them had the stomach for. And then the slow slide into afternoon drinking, the silences gradually warmed up by alcohol into bouts of pointless quarrelling that erupted into full-blown heated dispute and then the stony silence again as they returned to the pension, to the tatty communal lounge with its bar and TV and pool tables and faint smell of bleach and stale beer.

– This is a shit-hole, Lauren said.

– A year ago you would have loved it, said Nathan.

– That just shows how little you actually know about me, she said.

– Oh, fuck off, he said.

*

Two days before they were due to fly home, a notice was put up in reception: the students were coming back and everyone had to vacate the rooms. Provision had been made for their exit. They'd paid for the week, so rather than give them their money back, the people at the pension were offering to book the residents into alternate accommodation, a hotel near the airport. Nathan found the guy who had organized it all and asked if they could have an extra room at the hotel. Yeah, no problem. Our mistake, he said. The guy was very apologetic, but to Nathan and Lauren it was a blessed relief. Neither of them had the slightest desire to share any further proximity.

It was over, they said.

They both agreed.

The next day they boarded a bus that took them to a hotel near the airport. It was clean and modern and featureless, a square brick of concrete and smoked glass, not like the grand looming hotels in Wenceslas Square. The girl on reception crossed their names off a list, smiled, and held out one key.

– Two, Lauren said, – two rooms, please. She held up two fingers and pointed to herself and Nathan.

The girl nodded, yes. – Two room, she repeated.

– But that's only one key, said Lauren.

The girl frowned and held the key out to Lauren, jiggled it impatiently.

– *Jit nahoru*, she said. – *Jit nahoru!*

She was insistent and they were tired. Lauren took the key and stomped off, Nathan dragging the cases after her.

They found the room. It was a large lounge area with a double bed at one end. There was a TV and a small coffee table and a two-seater settee. A door revealed a smaller room with a single bed and wardrobe.

– OK, said Lauren. – Two rooms.

They spun a coin and Nathan got the double bed. Lauren took her stuff into the other room and shut the door. Nathan heard the bolt slide home.

He sat on the bed for a while and watched an ice hockey game on the TV until Lauren banged on the wall and asked him to turn it down, please, she was trying to get some sleep. He switched it off and went outside for a wander round. There was a market in a small square a few streets behind the hotel. Nathan bought a salami sandwich and a carton of juice then found a bar where he hunkered down with a beer for an hour so. He watched the people walk around, the girls and the couples especially. People walking hand-in-hand, some of them laughing.

What was their secret? Nathan looked for clues in their faces, their clothes, in the way they walked. Happiness. How did you do it?

He couldn't find any answers and after a while he stopped looking.

*

When Nathan got back to the room, there was a man sat on the edge of the double bed. He stood up quickly as Nathan came through the door. A small guy with lank chin-length black hair and a scruffy five-day growth, furtive looking. Grubby camouflage jacket, faded black jeans and heavy boots. Multi-coloured beads around his neck and wrist. He looked like a hippy roustabout, like someone who had just dropped off the back of a box-car.

– Hey, man, he said. – Whoa, this is all, like, a big mistake.

The man held up his hands in a placatory gesture. Nathan could see ingrained dirt on the palm of his hands.

– I tried to tell the girl but I guess I couldn't make her understand.

– Lauren?

Nathan went straight to the bedroom door and tried the handle. Locked. He banged on the door.

– Lauren? LAUREN?

No answer.

– Hey, listen man, I don't wanna cause no trouble, maybe I should just...

The man took a step forward but was halted by Nathan's jabbing finger and the violence in his voice:

– Don't you fucking move, pal. You just stay there.

Bang bang bang on the door again.

– LAUREN!

The guy launched into a long and rambling monologue about the girl giving him a key and he could see there was someone already here and how it was all a big mistake, man, but he couldn't make the girl understand and hey, listen, I'll just get out your way, I just thought I should wait for you to come back, see if we could figure this out, but hey man...

BANG BANG BANG.

From behind the door: – Alright, alright, fucks sake...

Nathan heard the bolt slide back and the door opened. Lauren stood there, fuddled with sleep.

– What the fuck, Nathan?

He grabbed her by the shoulders.

– Lauren! It's OK! You're OK, babe!

He pulled her into him. She tried to pull away, but he held tight on to her.

A voice from behind:

– Hey, listen kids, I'm gonna get outta your way, I apologize deeply, man, OK?

Lauren squirmed out of Nathan's grasp, pushed him away and looked at the man, who was almost crouched in subservience, head bowed, hands clasped together as if in prayer.

Then she looked at Nathan.

– Who's this? she asked.

*

Lauren sorted it all out. She called the woman up from reception and with the aid of a translation app on her phone established that the man – Craig, he was called – had been given the room in error and needed to be allocated another. That he had been sat quietly, waiting for someone to return. Introductions were formally made. Explanations established. A key was duly delivered.

Craig kissed it like a trophy, held it aloft.

– Kids, he said, – I can't thank you enough. If it weren't for you I'd be sleeping in the woods. Lemme buy you dinner tonight. Waddya say?

– It's a kind offer, but there's really no need, said Lauren.

– Lauren, please. Dinner on me. It's the least I can do.

Craig looked genuinely hurt. He turned to Nathan in appeal.

– Nathan? C'mon man. It's my last night; let me celebrate by buying my new friends some dinner? Huh?

– It's our last night too, said Nathan.

*

There was no one in the hotel restaurant except them. They ordered BBQ chicken and fries and a bucket of iced Budvar. All on me, kids, said Craig. He had showered and changed into a clean blue denim shirt with a faded T-shirt beneath that said LED ZEPPELIN. He was clean-shaven, and his hair was washed and combed back off his face. His fingernails and hands had been scrubbed. They ate their food and ordered another bucket of cold beers, lit cigarettes.

Craig told them that he was forty-seven-years-old, half Cherokee and currently lived in San Francisco. He said he had lived all over America, did odd jobs and seasonal migration work, drifting up and down the coast and across the mainland. He'd been married and divorced twice. A daughter who he never saw. He'd spent time on the streets, served time in jail for vagrancy and petty theft and then travelled to Europe on his release, sick of trying to make the American Dream work for him. He moved around mainland Europe, basically living off his wits. Sold concert tickets in Vienna. Picked grapes in Italy. Building sites in Spain and Portugal. Never stayed anywhere too long.

– No one likes a half-breed, he said, – not in Europe or America or anywhere, man. In America they call me a half-breed, in Europe they think I'm a gypsy. Well, you've been here a few days, kids, you musta seen how the gypsies get treated – like shit on a shoe, right?

– Yeah, I noticed that, said Nathan.

– Did you? said Lauren. – When?

– When we were in that gallery the day before yesterday. Those women. They threw them out, remember?

– Were those gypsies?

– Yeah. Well, I presumed so. They looked like gypsies.

– OK, Lauren shrugged.

– Right, said Craig. – That's how they do. Since I ran out of money, I been getting the cold shoulder everywhere I been, man. No room at the inn. Getting moved on by the cops. Ended up sleeping out in the woods. Then today I called my buddy back home and he gives me the good news – my insurance claim cheque hit the mat.

He slammed a fist into the palm of his hand.

– Been waiting two years for that shit to come through. Painting a house for this guy, fell off the roof and bust my arm. Couldn't work for six months. I had him wire me the dough. First thing I had was a big plate of stew and dumplings. Second thing I did was buy me a bag of sweet smoke. Third thing I did was rent a room. Figured I'd get myself scrubbed clean and then head to the airport, get back home. I checked in here and the girl gave me a key, but then when I saw the room and your bags unpacked and all, I figured it was some kind of trap and she was gonna call the cops on me.

He glanced around the bar, as though the cops already had them surrounded.

– Paranoid, right? But that's how it gets you, man, that's how it can get to you. She thinks I'm some kinda gypsy is what I'm thinking.

– But you're alright now, said Lauren.

– Thanks to you, Miss. You made everything OK. My new buddies, right? Lauren and Nathan! He looked from one to the other, beaming.

– Nathan and Lauren, he said.

He held his palm up to each in turn for a high-five. Nathan laughed and slapped his hand. Lauren hesitated and then, half-smiling, slapped his hand too.

– That's the stuff, said Craig. – Ain't we tight?

He raised his bottle.

– To good friends!

– Good friends, said Lauren and Nathan.

They clinked their bottles together then drained them dry. Craig reached into the bucket and popped the lids on three more.

– Good beer for good friends. They got good beer here, he said. He gulped down a long draught and smacked the bottle on the table.

– Alright, he said. – So what about you guys? You married, huh? Children?

Lauren laughed. – No, she said. – We're a long way off being married.

– But you been together a long time, right? I mean, I can tell by the way you are with each other that you been together a long time.

– How do you mean? asked Nathan.

– You're soul mates, man. I could tell that straight away.

Nathan shrugged into his beer. He didn't want to look at Lauren, didn't want to see what her face might be doing.

– And you spread that around to others, too, Craig went on. – That's the beautiful thing, man. That's the most beautiful thing.

– Yeah, we're just a pair of hippies, Nathan said. – Love and peace, man. He held up his fingers in a V and adopted a mock doped-out beatific expression.

Craig looked at him and didn't laugh.

– I mean it, man, he said. – I'm serious as shit. Hey, I'm an American. A *real* American, you dig? An original native son. I don't do jokes, man.

Craig pointed his bottle at Lauren.

– I mean, she's precious to you, right? She's the most precious thing in your life. Am I right?

– Well... yeah, Nathan said. – Yeah. She is.

– I can tell, man, said Craig. – I can tell.

Nathan took a drink. He could feel his face burning up. He glanced at Lauren. She was looking at him. She smiled and she didn't look away.

– It shines through, said Craig.

*

It got darker outside and they got drunker. The laughter grew louder. They talked about music and books and films and football (... he could have had a trial with Hull City, Lauren told Craig, but he got glandular fever...) and America and the UK and mermaids and deserts and ghosts and vegetarian cooking and dull jobs and Disneyland and then a uniformed guard wandered into the restaurant. He was a tall, heavily built man with a shaved head and a soft babyish face. He had a large black gun holstered at his hip and a black baton strapped down one leg. A chain and handcuffs hung at the back of his belt. Nathan watched him pass behind Craig, who was drunk and unaware of the other man's presence, listening intently to Lauren's story about being stuck on a rollercoaster at the age of seven in Florida.

The guard started chatting to the barmaid who was sat up on a stool, looking at something on her phone. She showed him the screen and they both erupted with laughter and Craig turned his head at the noise.

– Aw, fuck man, he said. He put his bottle down and kneaded his temples with his fingertips, squirmed down low in his seat. He starting muttering to himself, shot a furtive glance over his shoulder. The guard and the barmaid were both engrossed in her phone, oblivious to them.

– What's up? said Nathan.

– Fucking cops, man.

– He's not a cop, said Lauren, – he's a guard. Look, he's got, like, a logo on his shirt. He's with the hotel.

Craig shook his head.

– Guard, cop, they all got fucking guns, man.

– Hey, don't worry, said Lauren. – He's not interested in you.

She reached across the table and touched Craig on the shoulder.

– C'mon, don't worry, she said. – You have just as much right to be here as him.

– That's not how these pigs see things, he said.

Craig chewed on his thumb. Lauren continued her story, trying to engage him, but it was useless. Craig kept shooting glances over his shoulder and screwing himself further down into his seat.

Then the barmaid slipped down off her stool and disappeared behind the bar. The guard came strolling over to where they were sat and leant over the back of Craig, reached down to the table and clinked together fistfuls of empty bottles.

Craig stood up suddenly and knocked back his chair. It fell to the floor with a clatter. The guard stood back, surprised.

Craig gripped the edge of the table, swaying. He was very drunk.

– Step off, man, he said. – Step the fuck off, OK?

He steadied himself, then swung around and headed for the exit, but his hip knocked the table and sent a heavy glass ashtray and several bottles bouncing onto the floor.

– OK, OK, called the barmaid.

Nathan stood up.

– It's OK, mate, he said to the guard, – he's just a bit pissed.

The guard shrugged, his arms full of empty bottles.

– *Nyni se zavira*, he said. – *Zadne dalsi pivo*.

He jerked his head towards the door to illustrate his point before walking back to the bar to stack the empties.

The barmaid came over with a dustpan and brush and started sweeping up the broken glass. Lauren got to her feet.

– Let me help you, she said.

– *Je to v pořádku*, said the barmaid. – *Nebojte se. Ale my se teď zavírá. Ahoj! Ahoj!*

The guard was leant up against the bar, his hand on his stick, watching them. He looked bored.

– I think it's time for bed, said Nathan.

*

The foyer was bright and harsh after the subdued orange and brown gloom of the bar. Craig was nowhere to be seen. Nathan and Lauren got into the lift and pressed the button. The doors closed and they lurched upwards. Lauren fell against Nathan and he put his arm around her to steady her. They were both very drunk. He kept his arm around her and they leaned back against the wall of the lift and watched the numbers change. A large mirror took up most of the back wall.

– He was really scared of that guard, wasn't he?

– Yeah, that was weird, that.

– Do you think he's on the run?

– I don't know. Maybe.

Nathan started laughing.

– What is it? Lauren said.

– What if we get back and he's all tucked up comfy cosy in that double bed?

Lauren laughed.

– I'd have to get in with you, said Nathan.

– Steady on, said Lauren.

She pushed herself away from him and messed with her hair in the mirror.

– Remember when we first met and you had green hair?

– It wasn't green, she said.

– It was, he said. – It was green and blue like a mermaid.

– You're pissed, she said. – I've never had green hair in my life.

He considered that for a moment or two. Then he said:

– We're going home tomorrow.

– I know, she said.

– What we gonna do?

– I don't know, she said. – Let's talk about it tomorrow?

– Let's talk about it now, he said.

– Not now, Nathan, she said. – I'm too drunk. It won't come out right.

– Tomorrow then? He tried to keep the hope out of his voice.

– We'll see, she said.

The numbers stopped at their floor, the lift doors opened and they walked out together.

A Wasted Journey

We're playing *Gears Of War* and I'm telling Luke about my ride down; about the psychopath that picked me up. I'd been dying to tell someone as soon as it happened. Even as it was happening, I clearly remember thinking: no one will believe this. I can tell it properly now, though; now that it's in the past. I don't even have to exaggerate any bits. But I could make it all into one big lie and he wouldn't care either way. Luke's my elder brother and I can tell when he's not really listening.

*

I stood at the slip road that led onto the dual carriageway and held my sign up to the passing traffic: LONDON PLEASE. Thick black capitals on the back of a ripped-up Cornflakes packet. It was rush hour still, not yet 9 a.m., and no one was stopping. The low sunlight was behind me, bouncing back off the passing waves of metal and glass. I held up the cardboard for forty minutes or so, until the glare from the windscreens made my eyes begin to smart and I got fed up. I sat down on the grass verge at a safe distance from the traffic.

A hundred and twenty pounds in my back pocket. The train fare Mum had counted out of her purse for me this morning. The train I wouldn't be catching.

I sat and watched the cars and vans and trucks whoosh by for a while and then I broke into the pack-up that I'd made the night before. I ate two cheese and ham sandwiches, a packet of salt 'n' vinegar crisps and a finger of Kit Kat before I noticed the car stopped twenty yards past me. The rear lights flashed twice – on and off, on and off. Bright metallic blue, this car was. A low-slung sports design with silver wheel trims and neon yellow lettering across the back windscreen. The engine revved, impatient, the car almost vibrating with the music.

I quickly got my stuff back together into my bag, sprung to my feet and ran to the vehicle. The passenger window was down, and I had to stoop to peer inside. The driver dipped down the volume and leant across the seat to push open the door.

– Take you as far as Goole, alright?

Mid-thirties, I guessed, but dressed ten years younger; Day-Glo green polo shirt with a large horse logo, oil-stained jeans and grubby white Reeboks, Nike-ticked baseball cap. Small gold hoop though his left earlobe and a scruffy blonde goatee. He looked up at me; it was a rough face, but he didn't look like a psycho. I decided that he looked OK.

– OK, I said.

I limboed myself into the car, bunched my bag onto my lap and pulled the door shut. I leant back into the seat and felt hard beads move beneath me; felt myself tipping backwards until I was almost horizontal. I grappled with a lever down the side of the seat, managed to jolt myself into an upright position. The driver was grinning at me.

– You alright there, pal?

– Yeah, I'm fine, thanks.

115

– There's a handle under the seat if you need more room for them legs.

– No, I'm alright, ta.

– Put your gear in the back, then. Might as well get comfy.

The driver lifted the holdall off my knees and swung it onto the back seat before checking his mirrors and indicating back out into the flow of traffic. He moved straight across to the outside lane. The inside of the car was smart; imitation leather seats and a polished walnut dashboard studded with banks of winking lights and illuminated dials. I couldn't tell what half of them meant. There was a strong scent of vanilla and something sharper like aftershave or deodorant, some cloying artificial garage-bought combination. A small St Christopher dangled on a silver chain from the rear-view mirror. It was all spotlessly clean. You could tell he spent every spare minute polishing this car. You just knew it was his pride and joy.

He glanced down at my cardboard sign that had dropped into the passenger foot well. – London, eh? What you doing down there?

– Going to see my brother.

The guy nodded as if he had known this all along.

– Live down there does he?

– Yeah.

– Poor bastard, he said, and he laughed. Several teeth missing from the side of his mouth.

– Yeah, I said. He likes it there, though.

– I worked down there for a bit, he said. Strange set of cunts, I thought. Whereabouts does he live?

– St Johns Wood.

– Ah yeah, well that's the nice part, innit.

I just nodded yes, although I didn't know how true it was. It was the only part I'd ever been to apart from the usual sightseeing stuff when we came down with school last year. The Houses of Parliament, Buckingham Palace, Downing Street; that was the extent of my London experience. The only other time I'd come down was to visit with Mum and Dad and it had hammered down with rain all that weekend. We never ventured any further than the Indian Restaurant at the end of the street. I didn't know whether St Johns Wood was good or bad; I'd never been to any other parts of London. I didn't tell him that, though.

– Which part did you work in? I asked.

– New Cross, he said. – Right shit-hole.

– Whereabouts is that?

– South of the river.

– Never been there.

He pulled a face. – You don't fuckin wanna neither.

– Why? Is it not very nice?

– Like Preston Road minus the glamour.

I smiled. – As bad as that?

– Nearly, yeah.

We both laughed and then fell into silence, except for the rumble of the wheels on the tarmac beneath us and the gentle throb of muted music inside. The singer's voice sad and distant sounding.

The driver sung along under his breath. I recognized the tune from the sixth-form common room.

– This is Pink Floyd isn't it?

– Yeah, you into 'em?

– Yeah, they're great, I said. – Good head music.

I remember reading that in one of Toby's old copies of *The Word*.

The driver grinned his gappy-toothed grin.

– I'm glad you said that, he said. He leant across and sprung open the glove compartment, rummaged around one-handed, then pulled out a small rectangular tin, dropped it into my lap. The tin was gold coloured with a picture of a Red Indian on the lid, a grave-faced Chief in full ceremonial headdress.

– One already rolled in there, he said.

I prised it open and there was this single white cone-shaped tube nestled in a bed of tobacco. I knew what it was. I could see the furled blue cardboard at one end beneath the translucent paper. I removed the cone carefully from its amber-brown bed, brushing off clinging scraps of tobacco, taking care not to drop any bits onto the seats. This guy pulled open an ashtray from the dashboard between us and felt about in his jeans pockets, found a lighter, slung it across.

I'd only ever smoked weed once before, at Toby's eighteenth, and I'd been as sick a dog, much to the disgust of Toby and the hilarity of everyone else gathered in the kitchen. I'd ended up clinging onto the edge of the sink and covering his mum's dishes with regurgitated cider and chips.

The driver glanced across at me fingering the spliff. I think he thought I was being polite.

– Spark it up, he said.

I did as I was told; put the joint between my lips, held the flame up to my face and sucked gently until the tip caught and glowed red. I took back a tiny pull of smoke and exhaled quickly, not wanting to disgrace myself by spluttering or coughing. It felt OK though, not like the soapy chemical tang I remembered from Toby's kitchen. This felt smoother on the throat, almost sweet even. I tried another cautious drag and took a little more of the smoke down into my lungs. It was hot, but not harsh or unpleasant. I took two more quick drags and then handed the smoking cone carefully over, lighted end upright, like a miniature Olympic torch. He took a deep drag and held his breath for what seemed like an absolute age before blowing a stream of smoke out of the gap at the top of his open window.

– Yeah, New Cross, he said. – Right fucking dump that was. Good laugh, though. Good set of lads.

– How long were you there for?

– Oh, a good few months. All last summer. Doing all these flats up for this Turkish bloke.

– Like renovating them?

– Yeah, just a bit of re-wiring and painting and that. Knocking a few walls down. He had a few flats, all round there. All pokey little gaffs as well, tiny as fuck. But that's how they live down there, innit.

I just nodded like a dummy. My head was starting to swim and my body was feeling strange, almost like it was weightless, without any density or mass. I fingered the hard beads beneath my thighs. They felt impossibly smooth and round. Like tiny wooden planets, I thought.

– And the rents he was charging as well! Two grand a month, some of 'em, y'know.

I tried to think of how much Luke's flat cost. I knew that Dad paid a certain amount towards it every month but I wasn't sure how much. I knew it was enough to set him off moaning once a month when he opened the envelopes over the breakfast table, but I was fairly certain it wasn't as much as two thousand pounds a month. I tried to imagine two thousand pounds spread out on a table. I couldn't think what it would look like.

– Wow, I said.

– I know, nodded the driver. – Robbing cunt. He want a bad bloke actually, though. Good payer. Sorted us with some nice smoke an'all.

He offered the joint back across and I extracted it carefully from his fingers. I took a small puff and then a deeper one; tried to keep the smoke down longer like this guy had done. Toby says the longer you keep it in, the better it works. I tried to count to ten and managed five before letting it all go in a mad rush. It seemed to be endless, the smoke. It streamed out of the two-inch gap at the top of the window like steam escaping from a kettle. I could feel my jaw begin to slacken and I could feel the spongy firmness of the headrest at the back of my skull. It felt good, the headrest. True and solid. I took another two hits and then leaned carefully forward, tapped ash into the ashtray, handed back the joint.

The driver leant back and sucked, let the smoke leak steadily through his nose.

– What does your kid do down there then?

– What? I mean, sorry? It was like I could hear him, but his voice was coming from behind a sheet of glass or something.

– Your brother. What does he do in that big London?

– Oh... he's... he's at drama school. I had to struggle to think what the name was for the school. I was going to say acting school at first, but I knew that wasn't the right word.

– What, like an actor?

– Yeah. Well, learning to be one.

– Has he been on the telly?

– Oh no. Not yet. He's just doing the training.

– How do you train to be an actor then?

I racked my brains, but I couldn't think of an answer. I realized that I actually didn't really know.

– I don't know, I said.

– Love to do that, me.

– You would?

– Oh, aye. Fuckin love films, me. Oh yes, listen to that!

He turned up the stereo as a guitar solo lifted up from the music. It sounded like a jet fighter taking off, a giant metal arrow being fired into the sky. I looked out of the window for vapour trails above but saw nothing except high wide yawning blue, not a single scrap of cloud up there, not the passing silhouette of a bird even. I scoured the sky until my eyes began to blur, then settled back and watched the huge industrial units of the retail parks roll past as we travelled towards the edge of town; watched all the man-made buildings give way to railway sidings and towering piles of junk in the scrap yards until we hit the countryside, the wide flat fields of green and brown and yellow. Then I got the distinct impression that the car was not moving at all, that we were sat as still as a stone in fact, and everything outside of us was a speeded-up film streaming past in a steady smear of Technicolor, like a two-dimensional ticker tape unfurling around this static metal box that enclosed us, the hum of the engine and the hiss of the wheels fixing us fast to the unbroken white line that was being eaten up beneath the bonnet. I tried to concentrate on the road, fixed my eyes on the rear wheels of the car in front, but the wailing of the guitar seemed to pull me up from my seat by the stomach until I was rising up like a child's balloon, rising above the cars and the vans and the trucks and the thin grey ribbon of road below.

And then the spell was suddenly broken as the driver flicked up his indicator and swung over to the middle lane, the world outside lurching suddenly to the left, leaving my guts at the edge of the road and the rest of me staring blankly at glass smeared with the speckled blood of smashed summer bugs and the rainbow remnants of windscreen wash.

The driver was singing softly to himself.

Jesus. How could he smoke that stuff and drive?

He dipped down the volume. – Have you seen the wall? he asked.

The wall? My ears were still ringing from that guitar. Had he said 'the wall' or 'the all'? All the what?

Then I remembered the film. *Pink Floyd: The Wall.*

I could feel the breeze from the window cooling the sweat on my brow, but the rest of me was too warm. I shifted about in the seat. I could feel the sweat under my armpits. I wanted to take my jacket off, but the thought of fiddling with the zipper and the seat belt was too much to consider.

– The Wall, I said, yeah, seen it a couple of times.

I don't why I said that. I haven't seen the film at all. But I knew about it; I'd read about it in that Bob Geldof book and that was almost the same as seeing it for real, wasn't it?

– Ever watched it tripping?

– I haven't, no. Bet it's mad, yeah?

– Oh, aye. Right on top. I nearly fuckin lost it one time. Thought the room had turned into a fish tank.

I snorted with laughter. I couldn't help it. Everything he said sounded funny. The way he was saying it, more than anything. Like it was the most normal thing in the world. I looked down and realized I was holding this smouldering joint between my fingers again. I couldn't remember taking it back from the driver. I was worried that maybe I'd been holding onto it for too long. I took a toke and passed it back.

– A fish tank?

– Yeah, like a big fuckin aquarium. Thought me mate had turned into one of them fishes – what they called, them bastards that eat you alive?

– Piranha?

– Yeah, fuckin piranha. Thought he was gonna fuckin gobble me up, man. Big fuckin teeth on him like razor blades.

I couldn't help laughing, the way he came out with it.

– Oh, aye, but it want fuckin funny, man. His face was all over the shop, y'know, big googly eyes and that. Fins growing out the top of his fuckin swede.

I could see it; the slack-mouthed bug-eyed stare of some nameless fishy demon swimming towards me out of the depths.

– That's ace! I said.

The driver shook his head. – Not for him it want. Wellied the cunt with a golf club.

I had to cover my mouth to stop myself. I took a deep breath and asked:

– Was he alright?

– Was he fuck. Had to go to Infirmary.

Oh God, I just exploded. Uncontrollable shrieking laughter. Howling. The driver looked at me, passed over the spliff.

– Cut his big fishy head open, he said.

Oh, Jesus! Oh bloody hell! I laughed so much I started coughing, nearly pulled myself inside out. I wiped my eyes and managed to compose myself. Then I felt a sudden surge of panic. I didn't want him to think I was taking the piss.

– Sorry, I said. – That sounds awful. I didn't mean to laugh. I'm sorry.

He just grinned, this guy. – Nah, served him right, he said. He allowed a pregnant pause and then said, – Fuckin tropical man-eating cunt.

Absolute uproar, the pair of us. The car rocking with laughter as it sped along the motorway, the world outside bright and clear and glorious.

*

– Here you go look, I'll drop you here.

There was a large blue and white sign; a crossed knife and fork, a petrol pump, a bed, a cup of tea, a stick man in a wheelchair and a smaller white circle with a black car and arrow pointing down to a carpark ringed by tall hedgerows. I could see the roof of the service station above it, the red, yellow and blue Burger King logo and the beaming face of the KFC Colonel peeping above the bushes.

– Just walk round to the other side and stand on the exit road, this guy said. – Or ask one of the truckers in the services. That's what I used to do.

– Yeah, nice one, I said. – Cheers mate, brilliant.

I unfolded myself from the car and offered the joint back across the seats but he just waved it away. – Keep it for the road, mate. I'll roll another 'un. Ey, don't forget this. He reached into the back seat and swung my bag out onto the road at my feet. I nearly had forgotten it as well.

– Aw, cheers man, I said.

– No bother, he said, and he gave me this big wink. – Have a safe 'un.

He pulled the door shut, sounded his horn and wheelspinned off, Pink Floyd fading into the distance as he disappeared among the flow of traffic.

I watched him go, then picked up my bag and walked around the grass verge that ringed the carpark, sucking at the last remnants of the joint until I felt it burning my fingertips and lips. I ground the dog-end underfoot and headed across the carpark to the service station entrance. It felt strange to be out of the car; to be upright and walking, with the sun on my back and the concrete beneath the soles of my trainers. I felt good, like I was walking along in slow motion. The sharp 3D rush that I'd had in the car had been replaced by a kind of muggy dream state that seemed to saturate me like a warm and comforting mist. I felt as though I were gliding as I entered the service station, past the chattering lights of the fruit machines and the entrance to the shop with its brightly-stacked banks of sandwiches and CDs and magazines. I floated past the cash machines and the café and headed straight for the red and white counter at the far end where a girl with thick pancake make-up and a neck tattooed with black Chinese stars served me a Zinger Twister and a medium Seven Up with ice. I sat up on this high stool and demolished the Twister and drank my drink halfway down before I got the sudden urge to piss. I found the men's toilets and held my breath against the stink of disinfectant as I let myself go against the stark white porcelain wall. It seemed to go on forever. It was brilliant. It was like the best piss I'd ever had in my life. Like I'd never need to piss again. Then I washed my hands and shook them dry under a roaring tunnel of hot wind, before making my way back outside.

The sun was higher in the sky now and seemed to flood everything in dazzling white; the benches and the railings, the tarmac of the carpark, the tops of the parked cars. Even the grass verge seemed to shimmer with this bleached out light.

I checked the time: 10.18 a.m. I remember the numbers on my watch clearly. If I'd caught the train like Mum had said, I wouldn't have got into Kings Cross until at least 12.45. I tried to work out how far I was from London. The sign above the service station said Hartsmoor Services.

It dawned on me that I had absolutely no idea where I was.

Ring me as soon as you get there, Ben, she'd said. *Don't forget.*

I followed the road around to the petrol pumps and joined the exit road beyond. I positioned myself at what I judged to be a suitable distance from the entrance to the motorway, so the cars could stop in time. I dumped my bag at my feet and then I realized there was something missing: my cardboard sign. It was still sat in the passenger foot well of a metallic blue car full of weed smoke and music and now ten, twenty, maybe thirty miles away.

I stuck my thumb out and waited and, in fact, it was only ten short minutes before this small silver car pulled up. I opened the door and leant in: a man in his late fifties, gold framed glasses and grey hair and a beard.

– I'm going to London, I told him.

– Yes, said the man. He didn't look up or around. He kept both hands on the wheel and his eyes straight ahead.

I leant in further. – Is that alright? I asked. – London?

– Get in, he said.

I opened the rear door, put my bag on the back seat and closed the door carefully. Then I got in the front passenger side and pulled the door shut.

– Thanks very much, I said, and off we went.

The car was tidy inside, but there was a smell of coffee and stale food and something damp, almost, like old books. It was like he'd not opened the windows for weeks. It was small, as well, and I was all cramped up, my elbow jammed against the door handle and my knee almost touching the gear stick. I tried to tuck myself tight together into a ball, to occupy as small a space as possible.

– Where are you headed? I asked him, but he didn't answer me. I wondered if perhaps he was deaf or something. I repeated the question but again there was no response, just silence. Just the low murmur of the radio; some talk station, a man and a woman, but not natural conversation. It sounded like they were delivering lines, a play, perhaps, or some kind of performance. It sounded like some kind of staged dialogue, but the volume was too low to hear what they were saying or get any sense of what it was all about. I asked him again where he was going but he didn't say anything or even look at me.

I found myself talking to fill the quietness of the car, babbling away ten to the dozen, the words burbling from my lips like a steady stream of underwater bubbles. I talked about the weather and the day ahead and how nice people had been in stopping for me, until I gradually became self-conscious at the sound of my own voice and the marked lack of response from the driver and so my words just sort of trailed off until the silence just hung between us, hot and inflated like empty space.

– I've been on a wasted journey, he said. He spoke very quietly, little more than a mumble. I could barely hear what he was saying.

– What? You've been on a what? I said.

– I've been to Wales.

– Wales?

He nodded, all serious. – I went to see my Uncle, he said. – But he wasn't there. So my journey... was a wasted one.

He said this as though it were a matter of fact, not opinion. A fact of the saddest and gravest importance. I turned this announcement over in my mind, but I couldn't make any sense whichever way I considered it.

– Did he know you were coming? I asked him.

– It's very frustrating, he said. – Now I'm afraid I don't know what I'm going to do.

I was struggling for some appropriate reply. – Well... er... can't you ring him up? See where he is?

– I trained for six years to be an accountant, he said.

– Six years? Wow!

– Six years, he repeated. – I studied hard. Passed my exams earlier this year. My final exams.

– Oh, well that's good, I said. – Well done.

– But my Uncle wasn't there, he said, – and so that's six years down the drain. Six years of my life. I don't know what I'm going to do...

I didn't know either. I tried to make sense of what was being said, but my brain was still foggy and I couldn't find anything to cling on to among his words. Wales. An Uncle. Final exams. Six years wasted. The murmur of voices from the radio and the murmuring of this old man beside me.

– ... so my father said I had to go and see my Uncle and he would deal with me. But when I got to Wales he wasn't there. So... six years training wasted...

– Deal with you? I said. I realized that I was beginning to sound increasingly like an idiot, just repeating everything he said, but he didn't seem to notice.

– I borrowed some money from the firm, he said. – Inadvertently. Do you see?

– Er, no, not really, I said.

– I'm not a thief, he said, and I could detect a slight edge in his voice then, like he was getting upset. – Please don't think that, he said.

– Oh no, I said, – I didn't, I mean... I don't... I mean...

I didn't know what to say.

– I was going to put it back, he said. – All of it. But before I got the chance, I was discovered. My father. He found out what I'd done.

– Your dad?

– My father, yes.

I felt it then; the first jolt of real fear, as though I was approaching something dangerous, like the edge of a cliff or something. I could feel a creeping cold sickness at the bottom of my stomach.

– So, is it like... the family firm?

– No.

– Right... I'm sorry, I don't really follow...

– It's very simple, he said. – Unless I can prove to my father that I have been caned across my bottom, I will lose my job. Six years training. But my problem is, I don't know anyone well enough to ask them to do it for me.

He looked at me for the first time then, just a quick sidelong glance and I realized I had been leaning in close to hear him, he was speaking so softly; close enough to follow the ticking of the tiny black second hand on the face of his golden wristwatch; to smell the carbolic soap on his neck and to feel the warmth of his breath when he glanced around. I quickly shrank back into the seat and faced front, arms folded across myself. I felt suddenly hot then, when he said that, far too hot. I could feel the side of my face and neck flaring up red.

It's a joke, I thought at first. Just a sick and stupid joke, like at Toby's sleepover that time when Toby said his cousin had licked their Nana's cat out for a dare when he was pissed on MD 20/20 and everyone had said *Oh my God* and *That is fucking gross*, but at the same time we all knew that it was a lie; just something said for effect, to shock everyone and make us all gasp and groan with disgust.

– Cane you? I said, trying to sound like I was laughing, but I couldn't keep the tremor out of my voice.

– Until I bleed, he said. – But I don't know anyone.

Oh Jesus... I felt a sickness spread through me. Like I was full of cold, heavy rocks. I didn't know where to look. My eyes couldn't settle on anything and I could feel them filling up. Don't cry, I thought. Don't start crying, whatever you do. I could sense the driver snatching quick looks at me as he drove. I wondered if he was after money. Maybe that was it.

I felt the small fold of paper in my front jeans pocket, the money for the train fare that Mum had pressed into my hand not three hours previously. Felt the hard edges of the coins digging into my hip bone. But I knew deep down that he didn't want any money. This was something else, something different. There really *were* people like this in the world. This was happening. It was happening now. I became conscious of my body as I sat there, not two inches from this old man who wanted to be caned. I could feel the hairs prickling up on the back of my arms. I could feel the shape of my cock and balls in my jeans.

– Will you stop the car please, I said.

– I'm sorry?

130

– Stop the car, I said to him. – I'm going to be sick.

*

Luke isn't really listening. He just blasts away at the soldiers on the screen and doesn't say anything. I've already died. I put the controller down. My fingers are aching from all the shooting.

– Go on, then, says Luke. – What happened next?

– Nothing, I say. – I told him I was going to be sick and he just let me out at the next services.

– And that was it? Luke looks at me, disgusted.

– That was it, I say.

But that wasn't it. That wasn't it at all. I could have been dead. I could have been in the boot of his car by now, chopped up into little pieces. Or tied to a chair in a cellar with a gag wrapped round my face. Maybe I should have exaggerated it a bit, said I'd jumped out of the car at full speed or something. Made it more of a story. But he was a proper psycho. I don't need to make anything up. I think I handled it well. It could have turned out much different.

– Have you called Mum? You'd better call her and tell her you got here.

I don't say anything. I've got a hundred quid left, after the KFC and the Oyster card. Toby says you can buy weed from the guys on Camden Lock. You just walk past and nod at them. I'll see if Luke wants to go down tonight, get ourselves some gear and stay in and get stoned. I'll pay for it. I'll go by myself if he doesn't want to come. I know where it is from here. I looked it up on the tube map; it's easy. You can't get lost in London, and anyway, this is one of the good parts.

The Line-Up

She starts crying again.

Tony lies on the couch and listens to the noises coming from behind the bedroom door. He doesn't know how long she's been awake, or even if she went to sleep. He knows for a fact that *he* hasn't. Tony's been lying here all night, cramped up on this couch with his eyes closed and his head jammed wide open, scrambled messages from inner and outer space ricocheting around his brain.

Her noise, his silence: the soundtrack to their last three days.

It sounds like the tail end of something, though, this crying; muffled sobs into bunched-up sheets that dissolve into trembling hiccups and snot-choked sighs. Tony listens to her breathing; snatched and ragged at first, but then steadying and slowing, succumbing to the heavy depths of sleep.

Sleep, please, just... sleep...

Tony listens. All quiet now, except for the noise of traffic from the street below and a telly laughing away to itself in one of the downstairs flats. Long seconds pass. Silence, finally, from the bedroom. Heavy silence in the room. Tony can feel the vein pulsing in his temple. His mouth is parched dry. He thinks about trying to get up, going to the tap in the kitchen, but he doesn't trust himself to move through the gloom without knocking something over. This peace is fragile and precious. He opens his eyes and turns his head, tries to make the contours of the room appear from the gritty murk. Gradually, he sees the shape of things. The table and where he thinks the TV might be. The curtains. He thinks if he could get up he could move slowly and find the kitchen door.

He starts trying to tell his bones to move. Then a wail of fresh anguish from behind the door and Tony's heart almost leaps clean out his chest and he sits bolt upright, gasping.

The renewed bout of sobbing goes on for another five minutes or so, but seems like several lifetimes lived over. Tony lays back down and closes his eyes.

I can't stand very much more of this.

*

The sun really pours into this place first thing in a morning, belting through the pale blue bed sheet that's tied across the window. Tony twists around on the couch, the hot sunshine spreading across his back, tongue clacking around in a cotton-wool mouth. He's managed to kick the sleeping bag off in the night, and a blind fumble on the floor to retrieve it results in fingernails dipped in soggy ash and a glass of something spilt.

Bastard.

He clamps his eyes shut and tries to burrow his way back down among the cushions, twisting onto his front, his side and then onto his front again. It's useless. No matter how he arranges his tired bones, Tony can't escape the glare of the sun

That relentless bastard sun.

Tony thinks that he might as well get up, but as soon as his eyes blink open there's a brilliant white flashbulb stamped straight onto his retinas. Screwing them tight shut again only sends tiny grey circles exploding backwards into his skull. Tony grinds his fists into his eye sockets and then sits with head between hands until everything gradually comes wobbling back into focus: the patterned carpet swimming below him; the edges of the table; the telly to the left of the window; the radiators; the chairs; the blurred edges of the room beyond that. Tony can't see it properly, but he knows it's all still there.

He pulls himself upright, swings himself around and plants his feet on the floor. He feels alright, all things considered. His guts are a bit chewed up and his head is throbbing like a bad tooth, but generally he feels OK. He's fairly certain he's not going to puke, but his throat and mouth are sandblasted dry and there's an elephant standing on his kidneys. Tony needs to piss, desperately. But that means going through the bedroom.

There's an empty pint glass on its side on the floor, a dark flower of water blooming out onto the carpet. He contemplates pissing in the glass, but there's at least half a gallon of liquid aching to leave his poor swollen bladder. For one brief second, Tony considers pissing out of the window. He wonders what time it is, if it's early enough for the streets to be deserted still. He has a snapshot vision of passing pedestrians being showered with filthy yellow rain.

Jesus Christ, it's your fuckin flat man! Just get up, go through there and have a piss.

She's buried somewhere under the duvet. Tony steps softly around the bed and into the bathroom. He unfurls toilet roll down into the bowl and drenches it flat with a steady jet of urine. Then he fastens his mouth under the cold tap and gulps and gulps until he's gasping for breath.

As he leans against the sink, Tony stares blankly back at himself in the mirror: hair plastered with sweat across his forehead, skin like congealed porridge, eyes two bloodshot flowers. He looks like a week-old corpse dug up and dragged from its coffin.

Tony leaves the room without flushing, picks his shoes up, and leaves the flat — pulling the door shut tight behind him.

*

It's hot outside, not a cloud in the bright blue sky and the street is indeed deserted. So is the road at the top of the street. There's no one in the newsagents either, apart from Mr Kumar's eldest daughter cutting the twine from a fresh bundle of newspapers. Tony guesses it must be earlier than he thought. He gets a *Sunday Mirror*, ten Bensons and a bottle of Orange Lucozade.

He's halfway back up the road when the cop van pulls up alongside him, blotting out the sun and freezing him in its shadow. As soon as the blue and yellow squares slide into his peripheral vision, Tony's hand instinctively goes to his pocket; but it's too late now, they'll have clocked him. And besides, he knows he's clean, at least on the outside. There's still three days' worth of dirt inside him. Cheap booze, rough-arsed gak and copious amounts of weed playing stop-start with his bloodstream, fizzing away at his guts and fanning the embers that fall from the fireworks still displayed in the back of his skull.

Just don't look them in the eye.

135

A young, blonde-headed, baby-faced copper hangs out of the passenger window.

– Excuse me, mate? Wonder if you mind helping us?

– What with?

– We need men of your age group and answering your description for a police line-up. Take about an hour of your time and you get paid in cash. You interested?

Tony puts his hands over his eyes and squints into the shadows.

– How much do you get?

– Tenner. Fancy it?

– What if they pick me out though?

– Then you win the holiday.

The blonde policeman smiles.

– Sounds ace, says Tony.

– You fancy it then?

Tony thinks about the flat and what's waiting for him there. The sobbing and the screaming. The recriminations. The bloody battle renewed.

– Yeah, he says, – go on then.

Blondie hops out and opens up the back of the van. Inside is another lad who, rather alarmingly, does look similar to Tony – about six foot, dark hair, unshaven, tracksuit top and jeans. Except this lad has got a sports bag at his feet and looks like he's just emerged from the steaming showers of a gymnasium changing room, rather than a cold ditch by the roadside. For a split second the lad seems as confused as Tony. He looks like he's about to say something, some greeting or acknowledgement of their mutual likeness. Instead, he just gives a quick nod and looks away. Tony climbs in, the doors slam shut, and off they go, holding onto the sides of the seat as the van picks up speed.

Well, this is different.

*

The two policemen seem agitated. The van keeps slowing down and then speeding up again. Tony hears the driver say, – What time they wanna start?

– Half nine, says Blondie.

– Time is it now?

– Quarter past, nearly.

– Bastard.

The van slows to a crawl as they mull over their options. From where Tony is sat, he can see the driver's eyes in the wing mirror, scouring the street.

– Bollocks to it, he says. – William Booth?

– Yeah, fuck it, says Blondie.

They spin a three-point turn and shoot back up the opposite way, towards town. They roll up outside William Booth House and Blondie hops out. The driver keeps the engine throbbing, fingers tapping on the wheel. He hums a tune to himself as he waits.

William Booth House. The local hostelry for the homeless and dispossessed. The Sally Army. Tony thinks about the old lasses shaking their tambourines outside Prospect Centre at Christmas, the old fellas with their chests adorned with medals and swollen ruddy cheeks, blowing their last breath into proudly polished brass. *Come and join us, come and join us.* Tony's never been in William Booth – never slept there, anyway. Although he did nearly call on their hospitality one night, when a brutal week-long drinking session culminated in him getting filled in round town at about half past three in the morning. He'd managed to crawl as far as the benches at the corner of Mytongate, where he'd curled up in a ball and passed out until morning.

Tony sneaks another glance at the lad sat up the other end of the van. He looks like he's bobbed off; eyes shut, head tilted back. Tony thinks that the lad has got the definite look of him, there's no denying. It's not just the dark hair and the height, it's the physical shape of his face. Especially in profile: the slope of the nose, the long jaw-line; the downward turn of the mouth.

Jesus, he's the absolute spit...

Tony realises he's been staring like some sort of psychopathic stalker, so he turns away and forces his eyes out beyond the grille screwed across the back window. But the glare of the sunlight makes him feel nauseous and before he knows it, his gaze has been pulled back to the other end of the van.

Tony's unease mounts the longer he examines the lad's face. The bastard looks exactly like him, the absolute double. The cogs in his head start to crank into gear again, and before long, Tony has managed to convince himself that this lad is his very own long lost brother, that they were separated at birth and abandoned to different orphanages by heartless uncaring parents. That's it, thinks Tony, that explains everything. That's what all the yearning has been about, this nameless sense of loss that's haunted him as long as he can remember, this gaping chasm at the centre of his soul that's pushed him haplessly from one disaster to the next, right from the moment he was born. *I'm not a bad person*, Tony reasons, *not a hopeless waste of bastard space like everyone says I am. No, I've just been ripped apart from me other half and cast adrift, left to stumble through the world on me own.*

Jesus fuck! That's it! That's why I'm in this cop van. It was meant to happen. It's fate. It all makes sense now.

This notion elates him for a few glorious seconds, quickens his pulse and lifts his mood. Tony is flooded with relief. He feels whole again. He's found his brother. He fast-forwards their story in his mind's eye; imagines the pair of them walking out of the police station locked in deep discussion, repairing to the nearest pub to tell their respective life-stories, laughing over a table full of drinks in a sun-drenched beer garden.

But then the film reel in his head stalls and jams, quickly reverses. The dark clouds rolling backwards to block out the sunshine and Johnny thinks, *Oh fuck, no... that's not it... that's not it at all... this is not my brother... there's no magic missing half to make me better... no happy ending here... this is... this is all a set-up... a fuckin set up by the pigs... it's a conspiracy... a plot to eliminate me... no... and not just me... people like me... that's it... that's what they're doing... they're rounding up everyone that looks like me... slinging them in the back of cop vans and slamming 'em down forever!*

Tony looks at the lad again.

That's what I look like. That's what I look like when I'm asleep. That's what she sees lying next to her when she wakes up before me.

He remembers the time one Christmas when he was woken up by three sharp slaps across the face, her sat on his chest, pinning his arms to the bed with her knees. This was the day after she'd given him the money to go into town and buy presents and he'd spent all afternoon in the pub. And then the betting shop. And then the casino, desperately trying to win back the presents he'd drank.

The rear doors open and light floods in, jolting the Lad Who Isn't Tony awake. He and Tony both turn with hand-shielded eyes as a procession of men clamber into the van. Tony slides along the seat to accommodate the incoming bodies. They jockey for position as the doors slam shut and the van lurches off. One of the men cockles over as he's trying to set himself down, falls sideways, his hand on Tony's knee to steady himself.

– Sorry bro, he says.

They get sat down and shuffled along, all of them wedged up tight. Tony shuts his eyes. He can smell stale tobacco and strong deodorant. His guts churn and he feels sick.

No one says anything. They just cling onto the edges of the seat as the van pulls away and speeds up, the wail of the siren parting traffic as they fly through the city towards Priory Road Police Station.

*

The canteen at Priory Road smells of stewed tea and freshly scrubbed floors. Empty plastic trays stacked in front of fastened down servery shutters. Posters offering instruction or warning dotted along pale green walls. Radios crackle in the corridors outside.

The Line-Up are loosely assembled around the chairs and tables, a rag-bag collection of weather-worn clothing, ink-scarred limbs and rough, unshaven faces that gaze blankly around the room or down into newspapers or plastic cups of steaming coffee. Tony knows he's been lucky never to have been homeless; all the times he's been pelted out of houses and flats, he's always had a bird or a mate who'd let him crash. These blokes though, these blokes look like they're no stranger to dinner queues or communal sleeping quarters.

There are seven of them scattered across the canteen. Tony weighs them up, one after the other. As far as looks are concerned he thinks that none of them really fit the bill, not for the purpose of this line-up. The one opposite him, the youngest looking one, he's got the height and the dark unkempt hair, but his face is too full and rounded, too babyish with pink clear skin. There's a half-hearted moustache, a wispy lick of down that only serves to accentuate his tender years. Wispy Tash seems on edge, constantly shifting in his seat at the slightest noise from the corridors outside, his eyes jumping about like Lotto balls.

His immediate neighbour is a seasoned *al fresco* drinker some thirty years his senior, face a mass of ruptured vessels. A forest fire of acne rages around his cheeks and chin. To his immediate right, another countenance made ruddy by alcohol and the elements, this one fringed at the chin by a raggedy ginger beard, and split by a happy gummy grin. It is the happiest face in the room. It was like being selected for a police line-up was by far the best thing that had ever happened to this face.

Happy Face gurgles away to a morose looking fifty-odd year old with sad and heavy eyes that look down on densely tattooed hands that turn an empty plastic coffee cup round and round and round, picking it to pieces and flicking the bits onto the table.

The next bloke down is a lad in his mid-twenties with dead black beetle eyes beneath the brim of a cap. He's dressed in a grubby white Adidas tracksuit top and looks like any one of a hundred other young men you'd find slouched in the back room of a pub or banging the fruit machines in the town arcades. But there's something vaguely familiar about him as well. Tony searches his face for some clue but can't fathom it. The lad seems utterly detached from the entire company; sat back in his seat, arms folded, thousand-yard stare aimed beyond the walls and windows and everything else.

There are two more men on Tony's side of the table. The one nearest to him looks like an ageing doorman gone to seed. He lowers a shaven head over Johnny's discarded *Sunday Mirror*, muttering curse words under his breath as he flips over the pages. The progress of his outrage is followed with keen interest by the man on his right, an affable looking bearded giant of a bloke in a filthy red quilted jacket that's at least two sizes too small and thus strains to conceal the huge shoulders that roll with mirth and the big solid beer belly that shakes the edge of the table as he chuckles with delight at his neighbour's vitriol.

The last two William Booth men are at the table across the room, sat opposite The Lad Who Isn't Tony. One is an old geezer well into his sixties with a double-breasted de-mob suit and Bobby Charlton comb over. He looks like he's been locked in a cupboard in a council house for the last forty years. His mate is a skinny, cadaverous looking man in his late forties with a salt-and-pepper mullet and a huge pair of shiny black wrap-round shades. He looks like a rock star on hunger strike.

A sudden burst of muffled music, the first few bars of some Oasis guitar anthem. The Lad Who Isn't Tony digs into his trackie pocket and pulls out a mobile. He gets up from his seat and wanders over to the windows at the far end of the room.

– Alright? You get me text? Yeah... yeah, I know. Mad, innit?

He glances over his shoulder at the rest of the line-up and then looks out of the window as he listens.

– Yeah, he says, – yeah, no problem... soon as I'm out of here... yeah. Alright, laters.

He kills the call and pockets his phone, but doesn't return to the table. He stays where he is and looks outside, a black silhouette against the bright blue window.

Tony stands up and as soon as he does he wonders why he's standing up. He feels like he should go over to the window, go and stand with The Lad Who Isn't Him. But instead, Tony sits back down. He feels uncomfortable, ill at ease. Tony thinks he can smell himself as well, the sharp tang of salt as the residue of three bad days begins to seep from his body.

Tony folds his arms, crosses his legs, and waits.

*

– Can I just have your attention please, gentlemen?

Everyone looks round. There's a blue uniform at the door. He's holding a sheaf of documents in his hand and looks harassed.

– Lads, I'm really sorry but there's been a bit of a hold up. Nowt for you to worry about, just a few problems with solicitors. But it does mean we're going to be here a bit longer than expected. I do apologise.

He rubs a hand over his head. He looks like he wants nothing more than to fuck off home to a roast chicken dinner and a can of lager on the couch. He looks around the room.

– Anyone who wants to go home can do so. But obviously, we'd be grateful if you stayed.

– Do you get paid more money if you stay? asks Purple Face.

– Yes, says the policeman, – same again.

– Another tenner?

– Another ten pounds, yes.

– Spot on.

Purple Face leans back and rubs his hands together, obviously delighted at the prospect of a double helping of White Lightning and twenty Mayfair instead of ten. The copper casts another look around the assembled men.

– Everyone else OK with that?

– No.

Every head in the room swivels to the window. The Lad Who Isn't Tony walks back to his table and picks up his sports bag.

– I can't stop, I have to get off, he says.

The copper says that it's fine, not a problem and tells him to go down to the front desk and he'll arrange a car to take him wherever he wants to be dropped off.

A voice in Tony's head is telling him that he should go as well. That he should get in that car.

Maybe me and him are headed for the same part of town...

– Anyone else?

The policeman looks from face to face.

– No? Happy to stay? Yeah? Yeah?

He's looking at Tony. Tony can feel the panic swelling up inside him and he wants to say no, I'm far from fuckin happy to stay, constable, but the words get stuck halfway down his throat and instead of a reply, Tony gives him a nervous laugh and a non-committal shrug.

– Nobody? OK.

The policeman nods at The Lad Who Isn't Tony and they both disappear out of the door. Everyone else returns to their newspapers and coffee and muttered conversations.

Tony feels a sudden, hollow sense of loss, like the essence has been sucked out of him. He feels abandoned and vulnerable. Completely on his own.

I shouldn't be here. I shouldn't be doing this.

*

Tony tries to piece together the last few days. Fragments are emerging, half-remembered words and freeze-framed scenes floating from the fog clearing in his head. He remembers sitting with her in some city centre pub in the mid-afternoon, laughing and drinking, the sun winking off the bottles. She's shouting something to him over the blare of the juke box, her mouth hot against his ear. Then another pub – Bluebell, he thinks, then another that he can't remember the name of. And another one, this one with a table going over, and glasses smashing, and people rising from their seats and shouting. He remembers suddenly being outside and the darkness rapidly closing in and the lights of the marina shimmering around him. He's shouting her name. Then he's in some other pub or club, hanging onto someone's shoulder, babbling away ten to the dozen. And then a faceless, steroid-inflated monster in a black jacket and head-set has him by the shoulders, marching him down a long dark corridor. Then he's out into the open air again, pushed towards distant streetlights and headlights. He sees himself weaving between the traffic, aiming wild kicks at passing taxis. Last thing he remembers he's back at the flat, he's kicking the bedroom door and telling her she's a cunt, she's a fuckin cunt, she's a...

– I fuckin know you from somewhere.

Tony looks up.

Thousand Yard Stare is staring across the table at him.

Tony shakes his head.

– Don't think so, mate, no.

– Want you padded up with one of the Maguires in Hull? Dave Maguire?

– I've never been in prison in me life, mate.

He narrows his eyes and cocks his head to one side.

– Do yer know Tully? Sean Tullyson?

– No.

– Goes in Griffin?

– No...

– What about Raggsy and Phil Beanie and all that lot?

Tony's shaking his head and saying no, no, but the lad keeps firing names and pubs at him.

– Look mate, says Tony, – I don't know any of 'em, and I don't know you, sorry.

Thousand Yard Stare fastens his dead beetle eyes on Tony's and his mouth tightens into a sour smile.

– I know where I fuckin know you from, he says.

– Where then? says Tony, but Thousand Yard Stare doesn't reply. Just folds his arms and stares straight at him. And everyone else is staring at Tony now, all the rest of the merry men that make up The William Booth Roll Of Honour: Young Wispy Tash, Purple Face, Happy Gummy Grin, Tattoo Hands, Norman The Cursing Doorman, The Chuckling Giant, Bobby Charlton and Hunger Strike.

All of them looking at Tony.

– You don't know me, he says. – None of yer.

– Right, we're ready for you now, gentlemen.

Two policemen are at the doorway beckoning them all to stand up. Everyone rises and follows the officers down two flights of steps, through a long snaking corridor and past several glass-fronted offices and through three more doors until they arrive in a small stuffy room with pale green walls and no windows.

A door at the far end of the room opens and The Suspect walks in; about five foot eleven, unkempt greasy dark brown hair, black jacket, dark blue jogging bottoms. He's flanked by two other police officers and a bespectacled man in a dark grey suit carrying a black folder. The Suspect's solicitor, Tony assumes.

One of the uniforms steps to the suspect.

– OK, he says, – as we discussed: have a look at these gentleman, and tell me if you have any objections to any of them appearing alongside you in an identity parade.

The Suspect looks at his solicitor and then at the copper.

– Are you for fuckin real? he says.

– You can choose three to eliminate, says one of the other policemen.

The lad walks around the room examining each of their faces in turn, sliding his eyes up and down.

– Him, he says, pointing to Bobby Charlton. – And him. And fuckin him an'all, he says, indicating The Chuckling Giant and Hunger Strike, who's now removed his eyewear to reveal a pair of impossibly pinned pupils, like black grains of sand floating on pale blue swimming pools.

They leave with a police officer and the men are then asked to form a line. Tony attempts to move, but realises he hasn't got the mental energy required to choose a position for himself. To move in any direction seems too loaded with potential significance, whether accidental or intended. So Tony simply stands stock still, sweating like a dray horse, and lets the line form around him, Thousand Yard Stare to the left, and Young Wispy Tash to the right.

– I'm far from fuckin happy with this, says the Suspect.

– Don't worry, we'll deal with it, says his solicitor.

A police officer asks The Suspect to choose a place in the line-up and after a couple of seconds, he elects to stand between Tony and Young Wispy Tash. They part to accommodate him and then the line-up stands straight, looking directly ahead as instructed.

They stand there.

It's too hot in here. And I'm thirsty. I can't swallow, I can't breathe.

Tony licks the sweat from his top lip and sucks down salty saliva.

– OK Jeff, says one of the coppers, and a colleague turns and exits, returning a couple of minutes later with a hard-faced middle-aged woman with a helmet of steel grey hair and thick bottle-bottom spectacles.

– Take your time, says a policeman. – Be sure.

She starts at the far end and works her way slowly down the line; past Purple Face and Happy Gummy Face, past Tattoo Hands and Norman The Doorman. Up to Young Wispy Tash.

Tony's right foot has gone to sleep. He flexes his toes inside his shoe and his entire foot tingles with a million tiny explosions, the nerve endings slowly coming back to life. Tony wants to raise his foot, shake it about to wake it up properly.

The Witness moves to The Suspect. She looks him up and down, and then glances across at Tony. Her eyes widen behind her glasses and she takes one step backwards. Tony looks back at her. He can see his own face reflected twice, one in each broad curved lens of her spectacles.

Wow, look at that. There's two of me.

He closes his eyes and waits for the hand on his shoulder.

The Artist

... and me bastard head is banging and I can't find me pencils, where's me pencils? ... can't seem to get nowt going tonight... place needs a bloody good tidy up, is what it needs... Christ, and I wish he'd give it a rest on that bloody wall as well. It's the same every night, tap-tap-tap, all through the teatime news and *Emmerdale* and *Coronation Street* and the late night film as well, and him, what do they call him? That American fella with the long face? Nicholas Cage. Yes. Him. Thank you. On and on and bloody on. Relentless. Can I hellers like concentrate, no matter how loud I crank up the volume, there it is in the background, sneaking through every gap in the action, tap-tap-bloody-tap, like Chinese pissing water torture... no chance of me following this film now, lost the thread six scenes ago. So bollocks to it, I'll get on with some drawing. Hard enough concentrating anyhow with this Nicolas Cage mumbling his lines and all the other side-line characters popping in and out of the action, God knows who any of these are meant to be, none of it fits together... you can't make head nor tail of it, none of it. Why can't these American actors talk properly? I thought it was just me going deaf, but it's these, this lot, every modern film they have on nowadays, they all talk with their mouths clamped tight shut. Like him, now, listen –

huh muh hmm huh huh... something about a car... muh huh huh, yeah man, yeah... mutter mutter mutter... sat in a car now, two of 'em, Nicholas Cage and somebody else. Some bloke with a ponytail. Load of bloody rubbish. He takes the same part in every film he makes, this fella ... huh muh hmm huh... yeah man, yeah... can't understand a bloody word... and then that bastard next door tap-tap-tapping away over the top of it all...

... ah, yes, me pencils, there they are, underneath the night paper... still got half of that left to read... I like to save it, leave it for after, though... so... take me pencils out and do a bit of drawing. Spread me work out across the desk. Well, half me work; the other half's left trailing on the floor. I'm working from memory, here. There's too much stuff on me desk and under me desk and under the bed as well, piles and piles of paintings and drawings and bits of writing, books full of all sorts. Poetry and stories and sketches and stuff. Poetry, mainly. I like poems, they're easy to do. You can bang a poem out dead quick. Boxes and boxes and carrier bags full of all sorts. No more room in the cupboards to put any of it. Fire risk, they said. This is what we have to put up with. This is our cross. Fucking ignorant they are, half of the bastards working for this council. Most of 'em, anyway. She was alright, that lass who came round... but I'm not interested, I told her, I just wanna be left a-bastard-lone. Bet I know who called her, an'all...

... oh, bollocks to this fella. Mr Mumbles. American shite. Turn the sound on the telly down and put Stevie Winwood on – *Arc of a Diver*. Brilliant album. Love it. *Higher Love*. That usually does the trick when I need to sail away. Bring me a higher love. Yes. Thank you... so... where was I? Music and drawing. Yes. Been working on this one for a few weeks now... big epic landscape in dark dramatic colours, a scene at night with a lake and trees and mountains in the distance and a little black cottage on the shore, smoke curling up from the chimney. I need some smoke. What colour is smoke? Yellow? No, grey... aye, that'll do it... pale smoke. I'll have to save the yellow for the windows, do 'em like little dots of yellow. Coz if there's smoke coming out the chimney, there must be someone home, mustn't there? Nice little cottage, inky black, cuddled up tight against the mountains. That's where I'm gonna live, in a little house like this, somewhere out in the wilds... Canada, that looks a good bet. I could go abroad... I could go anywhere... go to Canada, up near the mountains, up where the air is clear. Live near a lake, a big stretch of water, all still and dark and smooth under the moonlight... something smoother... what was it? Something smoother happens. A thing on the telly, an advert years ago for ginger beer or ginger ale or whatever it was... BASTARD! What was it? Ginger ale and scotch on the rocks... long tall glass... a proper drink that was, oh aye, not like this pissy white wine, gives me gut-rot, this stuff... yes, by Christ, Canada. That's me. Or New Zealand, that's where they did *Lord Of The Rings*, it was on a programme one night... an interview with the director explaining why they did it all round there. Shot it all round there, they did. The scenery. The mountains... I never knew New Zealand looked like that, never considered the place, really. Can't recall it ever coming up. Australia, people used to talk about that, yes, but not New Zealand. But it's on the agenda. It's a possibility. Or maybe Wales or somewhere nearer to here, if money's a problem. Maybe Scotland or Ireland. As long as there's mountains and water and it's miles away from every other bastard I'm not bothered...

... stopped in Wales for a bit in the seventies, me and Hippy Joe... which sounds like a made-up name when you say it now, but he was a proper hippy, like, a naturist who talked to ants and lived in a treehouse... and a fella called Arthur Prendergast and the other one, who was he? Some sort of relation, his younger brother, I think... step-brother, maybe... can't recall his name, off-hand. He was a tailor, I remember that, Saville Row, in London... back when that actually meant something... back when they were at the top of their game. Oh yes. You knew you'd arrived if you could score a made to measure suit from Saville Row. He had a few bob is what I'm saying, this Arthur's brother. Step-brother, I mean. Nice kid. Can't think what he was doing hanging about with that crew... with all us lot... us load of drop-outs... squatters and bloody barb heads... he had his own flat in London, the nice part, up near Hampstead... anyway, it was Hippy Joe and Arthur and his step-brother and a few others... Little Nelly, she was there, she was one of 'em. All of us in this farm-house in Wales one summertime. The seventies, mid-seventies this was... remote place, man, nothing around for as far as the eye could see. But beautiful, yeah? Just endless fields dotted with sheep and stone walls rising up the hills and then these big purple mountains hanging there in the distance. And no one around, no other houses. Just endless paths through green fields and bits of woodland. Nearest village a twenty-minute drive away, I think it was... we used to take it in turns to go down for bags of booze from this little shop...

... this farmhouse place, it belonged to some rich fella that Joe knew, some blue-blood type with a family fortune... I remember Joe telling me his name and me going oh aye, yeah, I've heard of him... can I bollocks remember it now, though... Henry or Harry something... Harry... no that wasn't it... oh Christ, what was his bloody name? He was well known at the time, this fella, his name all over the papers, who was it? BASTARD, this bloody memory, this...

... tap-tap-tap...

... anyway, this Henry or Harry or whoever he was, it was his house. Or one of his houses. I don't know whether he knew, like, if he knew we were all there that summer... but what a place, man. One fine time we had us there, oh boy, picking mushrooms and wandering about the fields. By Christ, we had some fun, yes, endless days and nights of it... this farmhouse with a big open fire, and a big wide wooden table. It was all guitars and dogs and pots of mushroom tea on the stove... drinking wine and home brew and whatever... marvellous time we had, getting smashed in the countryside, getting deep into the landscape, into the paper... into the past... I'm there, man... my hand is a pencil...

... I saw in the paper how they've done up Ferens and they're wanting local artists to submit their work... didn't say if there was any money involved, though... there should be though, shouldn't there? They should pay local artists same as they do anyone else... mind you, first thing I'd do with any money is get me bastard glasses fixed. I get headaches staring at the paper, this white paper, it hurts me eyes. I have to shade it all in, fill in all the white space with colour and shade... I'm into me pencils at the minute... I like splashing the paint around, thank you, yes, but pencils are more the job for close-up work on a night, when the light's poor like this... and that bloody paint gives me headache an'all, the smell of the stuff for one thing, I can't be having that... it gets so you can't breathe, makes your head throb with the fumes and what with that and me broken glasses and all the banging and shouting outside and all that bloody thump-thump music they play on a weekend across the street and that bastard next door with his non-stop tap-tap-fucking-tapping...

... dear Christ, dear Christ, it's more than the bastard human mind can bear... stroke and scribble and shade, fill it all in, near and far, the mountains in the distance... the purple headed mountains... but no, this is more of a mauve, coz these pencils aren't as good as the last lot I had, the ones I had on Orchard, they were smashers they was, but they got lost when they shifted me... all done in a rush it was, bang, one day after dinnertime, just got slung a handful of plastic bags and told to hurry up... half me things went missing, loads of CDs and books and bits of me art and writing and letters and God knows what else... them bastards on the council, they're not bothered, you put a complaint in but do they listen, do they care, do they fuck... so... put a stream in, a stream leading to the lake... put a bridge over the stream, little stone bridge... now let's have some people stood on the bridge throwing sticks into the stream, two figures, like me and Nelly that time... I wonder if the council would pay for me to be in that exhibition? Or they might have dealers up from London... a cheque for one million pounds? Don't mind if I do, very kind of you, sir! Ha! They know a good thing when they see it, them London fellas... and that'd be me all set up in me London penthouse with me bevvy of exotic beauties and a giant tropical fish tank running the length of the wall, floor to ceiling, all silver and blue bubbles, striped zebra fish and angelfish darting about and neon fish and starfish and shells from the Indian Ocean... and I'd be there, stretched out on me sheepskin rug with that Madonna and Katy Perry and whoever else wanted to drop by, everyone welcome! Open house! Come on in ladies, a bucket of champagne on ice and a big cigar... but no champagne for me, no Canada Dry ginger ale and ice and scotch, oh no no no, them days are gone, no hard stuff for me anymore, sends me dingy. I'll stick to me white wine and soda thank you, yes... but the lasses, oh, the lasses could have as much as they wanted... another bucket of Bollinger, Miss Jolie? My pleasure madam! Help yourself ladies, plenty more where that came from... and the view from me window, the lights of the city stretching out below me for miles and miles, enough to snatch your breath away, all the buildings and signs lit up in neon and the red tail-lights of planes flying in from all over the world... where am I? ... Los Angeles, oh yes, and that's just for starters... Canada, Wales, New York... penthouses all over the world... all paid for by me paintings... I'll be there, L.A. man, with Nicholas Cage as my servant... what's that you're saying, Nick? ... you've got your sound turned down again, but don't worry, I can't understand a bloody word you're saying anyway...

... tap-tap-tap...

... Morse code, must be bastard Morse code... birds in the sky, bluebirds and swallows and geese in a V, all flying off to wherever they go for the winter, somewhere warm... this sky is not blue... well, not sky blue, more like gun metal blue, a blue stroke grey stroke blue strokes of the pencil and oh Christ, I never get no one coming to see me anymore, not had a soul to the door since that lass from the council, I've not got... I've not...

... oh, that's Stevie finished... I didn't even hear him leave... what an album that is... still in me top five of all time along with Frank Zappa and Average White Band and the first Roxy Music album and Ian Dury's *New Boots And Panties* and loads of others that got thieved when they shifted me off Orchard... fucking thieving bastards they are, you can't have fucking ANYTHING oh fucking STOP IT...

... stop... it...

... stop... what can I put in here? ... I've drawn the house too little to put people in and the birds above are too far away... it's all looked at from a long way away, this picture... the perspective of it all, like... this is what I've come to realise... if I'm going to have people in there, they'll have to be matchstick people like the couple on the bridge... Pink Floyd... no, I'm not in the mood for that now... Squeeze! Oh yes, oh boy, great band... or maybe the radio... they have some good programmes on now and you can get them all on the telly, on Freeview, BBC Radio 4, they have plays on sometimes, plays, interviews, all sorts of stuff...

... I think I'll have a face in this anyway... a big giant face looming over the mountains... it's my drawing and I can have who I want in it... those clouds up there, they look like what? ... Shakespeare's severed head on a dinner plate... I'll draw him, yes, Shakespeare... no, a jester peeking over the mountain tops... a jolly jester with a laughing face and bells on his hat and one of them sticks... what do they call them sticks? ... anyway, a tickling stick... no, behave yourself... that was that other fella, him with the hair all sticking up and the big teeth... what did they call that fella? ... anyway, a jester to entertain him, so at least old Shakespeare can have a laugh while his head is sizzling away on a hot plate... YES! the hot plate, the hot plate, Jesus, yes, that's what happened... I remember now... we were doing hot knives over this stove while Nelly was cooking up a big pan of stew and she was laughing at summat I said or summat Joe had said and she was drunk and doubled up with laughing and her hair dangled in the stove and it all caught alight and we were all too drunk and stoned and hysterical to help her... oh Jesus, and I swear there was one brief second when she seemed to be laughing an'all, half her head on fire and she's screaming with laughter, but within half a heartbeat they were proper bastard screams, screams of pain, like an animal, it sounded like an animal, terrified... someone emptied a bottle of wine over her head and batted it all out with a jacket or a blanket or summat... but she got burnt, oh Christ, a few nasty marks on her face and neck later, when I saw her... a few days after that... I remember a white bandage wrapped round her head... I remember... Oh, Nelly... all that lovely hair she had, blonde hair, almost yellow, like the edge of the sun behind these mountains... blend the red in with the yellow... make it orange... amazing what comes back to yer... all that time ago in that farmhouse... days and nights...

... this bastard tapping...

... the police came... I remember I'd woke up that morning and spotted them through the window, a line of cop cars crawling towards the house from high up in the hills... little black and white ants in a convoy... yeah, that looks good, a line of police cars coming down the big mauve mountain... little Nelly with her hair on fire... she got took away for I don't know what... can't remember what they charged her with... but that Saville Row fella, he had a load of gear... barbs, I think... we were all on them barbs... he got, what? ... three years, I think... this was back in the seventies, man... I did try warning them, all of them. I went from bedroom to sleeping bag to wherever and I said hey, look, it's the pigs, I'm bloody serious, here they come... and Joe, he just laughed at me, man, that long joker's face laughing up at me from the sleeping bag like it was the most hilarious fucking thing he'd heard in his life... anyway, I took off, got me few belongings together double-quick and legged it out the back way, right up into the mountains... oh boy, these mauve topped mountains... Nelly... she could come to see me... I could look for her on Facebook and send her an email and she'd come, I know she would... or Hippy Joe, come to that... he was meant to be my best pal, my oppo... hang on though, didn't he get lifted? ... I think I remember someone telling me later, sometime later when I was back in FUCKIN HELL THIS MEMORY these new tablets they've got me on, like a yo-yo I am to these people, a play-thing, trying this and that and the next thing, and they haven't got a fucking bastard clue what they're doing, none of them...

... tap-tap-tap...

... Miles Davis, *Kind Of Blue*... yes, thank you... absolute stone cold classic, turn it up, blank out that tap-tap-tap Morse code bastard and get carried away by Miles and his horn, man... Nelly, where are you, what you doing and did your yellow hair grow back, Nelly? ... I draw Nelly with her hair on fire running towards the lake, running to put her burning golden head out in the black Welsh water where I wandered for about, what, three days or so as I remember... three or four days and nights... probably just wandered round in a big bloody circle, boyo... I found a cave... draw a cave, black on mauve... put a cave up there in the mountainside... I remember that, how dark it was on a night time... I had a bottle of whisky with me to keep me warm... but it was summertime, I wasn't that cold... it was OK... I got as far away as I could from the coppers and all other signs of human life... I drank from streams, and food... well, I never used to think much about grub in them days. I'm the same now... I can go days without eating, just a bit of toast does me... I was never much one for the culinary experience or whatever you want to call it... the cuisine side of things... I was always a drinker, that was my game, food was always second to drink... Martini, that was the one... oh boy yes, a bottle of Martini for breakfast, anytime, anyplace, anywhere. But not here, no more, no, no more, no no no no, just a glass of wine or two on a night time now... it's not too bad this stuff, not bad for three quid a bottle anyway, well, three pounds thirty I suppose, three for a tenner. Not that bloody Martini, no. That's where I went wrong last time, that time I...

... time I changed this pencil... this one is worn down to the wood... going blunt, a flat edge, just rubbing at the paper now, making a mess...

... tap-tap-tap...

... I wonder if he's half as twisted as me, this bastard next door... or maybe he's in pain... dot dot dot, dash dash dash... save our souls... like these birds in the sky I'm putting in, short dashes, short pencil strokes, little black scars on the blue... dash dash dash... let's put a flock of birds in here, a massive teeming cloud of black V-shaped starlings or sparrows or crows or Jesus Christ any birds, any type of birds... but not the pigeons, there's thousands of them bastards hanging around... and the ducks, yes, the ducks, but they don't count, they can't get up and fly, they can't get off the ground... yes, I'll put a flock in here, in this picture... a flock of geese rising off the ground as one, but in the picture they'll be tiny black V-shaped scars flying away... but after a while everything is too much black and I need some more colour to soften things up and there he is, Nicholas Cage in his black T-shirt and his long face and his mannerisms... the way he throws himself around... he's there with the sound turned down... this picture... it's just occurred to me... I can make it daybreak in this picture... red sky in the morning, angel's warning or whatever they say... I could make it like that, like an angel's dawning. Red sky at night, Angel Delight. Nicolas Cage is an angel... I think I've seen this before... something to do with angels... I can draw an angel rising up....

... tap-tap-tap...

... oh my God, I am so very very lonely, I am so lonely, God... I don't even believe in you and I'm telling you I'm lonely, God, because no BASTARD ELSE WILL LISTEN AND THERE'S NO NEED THERE'S NO

... no no no, stop it, rise above it rise above it rise above it... like this luminous woman with her outspread wings rising from behind the mountains, this... this...

... tap-tap-tapping...

... I should just say summat to him, anyhow... if it carries on much longer I will definitely say summat, I'll go round and say summat, I can't carry on like...

... OK... so now it's sunrise over my lake and the cottage... well, that must be a morning fire, so I would say if they've lit a fire, this couple... it will be a winter's morning... I wonder if this couple are going to spend Christmas together in this cosy cottage, cutting their own wood and digging frozen spuds out of the snow... can you grow potatoes in winter? ... Surely you can, you just need a decent spade... you just need to keep digging away, like me with this pencil, I'm rubbing it away here, scrubbing, because I want to make this sunrise glow off the page, I'm scrubbing yellow into red and it's working it's working, it's working...

... tap-tap-tap...

... I can't afford to lose my temper anymore... I walked down off that mountain in Wales three days later, I got a ride to the nearest town... I can't remember the name... began with a C, I think... not Cardiff, not a place as big as that... anyway, I was proper unkempt and stinking and still tripping I suppose, what with the past few weeks and what we'd all been up to, this big pot of mushroom tea... I never said a word to anyone, never grassed anyone up in me life, not now and not then... this was all in the seventies, this, when I was...

... tap-tap...

... JESUS! HALLELUJAH! He's STOPPED! ... A miracle! ... Peace at last... my fucking head was about to go pop... oh, thank you, sweet Jesus, thank you for this silence, this sacred place... all a man needs is a quiet place to go about his work... to get his head down and get things finished... this picture won't be finished tonight though... doesn't matter... you can't rush a masterpiece... eyes are hurting now... this bloody light... need to get me glasses fixed... but when it's ready, I'll send it in to Ferens and I'll go down to the exhibition... it will be a nice day out... and then they'll see what I can do, all of them, everyone on that council, all those fellas in London and maybe Nelly will see me on the telly or in the papers, and she'll go oh look who it is, and she'll get in touch and we'll...

... tap-tap-tap...

RIGHT, YOU CUNT...

162

Hospital

Dear NHS, you are driving your users mad with this constant bleeping. And the lights... Jesus, how can we sleep beneath this canopy of UV? I have headphones and at least the radio is free. Could you please play a request for Sleepless of Spring Bank, trapped in an electric blue cocoon with a clamp on his leg? Please play anything by Snorey Norey and The Throat Rattlers.

I know my name and date of birth off by heart.

The school dinners are magnificent. Jugs of lukewarm water and a lofty view of distant ribbons that pelt with traffic even at 2 a.m. Children of the night. Soft rock anthems filling cars. God, I hope I never become a heroin addict. What hard work that must be.

That clumsy youth who banged my wheelchair in the X-ray room...

I wonder if I could stay awake for the full twelve weeks.

I bet the sunrise looks glorious through that full-length window. I wonder how many times I'd have to launch myself until the glass shattered and I was falling through the air, grabbing at damp night sky, framed in a halo of tiny diamonds.

It is taking all my effort of will not to royally kick off in here.

Try to transcend petty fury and discomfort though, and arrive at calm detached tranquillity. Rise to meet it, bound in white and blue sheets and entombed in trailing wires under a blazing electric sun. Peter at the night class told me not to use imagery like that, shards of light. I don't like that, he said. He's right, of course, a shard of light is a lazy crutch to lean on, some weak fumbling for a vague sense of mystic grandeur. This is why people pay good money to go on them courses...

I can hear a very old woman crying out in pain somewhere to the left. It looks strange, writing it down like that, using those words. Crying out in pain.

The only light in here is electricity and lack of light, lack of clarity.

I refuse to take drugs to make me go to sleep.

I am curious to hear what 3 a.m. sounds like in this box of propped up life.

I wish that cunt in the bed opposite would get some headphones.

*

All human discomfort is registered in the brain and it is very easy to fool the brain. A nurse told me a trick – if your leg itches beneath the cast, scratch the other leg on the corresponding spot. And, miraculously, it works. You can mislead yourself with this very simple move. I asked if it was OK to slide a knitting needle down there to scratch, but this was met with a mock-horror, no no no! Risk of infection! But what about risk of insanity? Harder to treat or cure. Bigger drain on the system. One of the other nurses has laryngitis, she sounds like a talking doll when the batteries run down.

Choice of three different pies for dinner. I'm gonna have to watch it in here, I'll be going out in a wheelbarrow. Anyway, the days in here are great; a man comes round with a trolley full of newspapers and chocolates, another lady wheels a tea tray round, someone asks you your name and date of birth every twenty minutes or so, probably to remind you of your continued mortality.

Time fairly gallops.

Later on, another nurse is going to show me how to inject blood-thinning drugs into my stomach. This is a new and delightful development. Hopefully, I will overcome my distaste of needles in time to get a raging smack habit to ease me through my seventies; just bang up and drift off into the arms of Jesus or Jah or Buddha, whoever will step forward first to catch the body.

This nurse, she says that her hairdresser won't let her have her hair cut short. Her own hair. This is what she tells me.

I'm tired and I'm struggling to take all this on board...

*

Jesus and the flamingo and the lights of the city outside again. I found a Book of Gideon in the bedside drawer. Spent most of the evening reading Murakami, some of it interesting, some of it not. Why am I being kept in here? Blood clots?

I can hear whispering in the corridor – your daughter just rung... I can't put the lights out just yet, I'm afraid... yes, I know it hurts... yes, I will do, soon...

If they catch me with my illicit phone charger I'll be for the chop. PATs testing requirement they said, but there's wires hanging from every bed. The tremulous wail of the elderly and hurting. A cup of tea? Do you have sugar in your tea? This is the national medicine, Britain's lifeblood. How about a Horlicks? Don't tell that fella anything, he'll write it all down and use it against you later.

I am keeping myself awake to watch a football match I have no interest in. When will I learn to focus my energies on things that really matter? Can you feel me touching that?

Someone came with a big bag of fruit whilst I was asleep, tons of it, enough vitamin C to rid an orphanage of scurvy. I woke up to apples and pears and oranges and bananas and blueberries and grapes.

I keep thinking about Gareth. There was a passage in that Gideon Bible in Welsh – well, in all the languages, but it was the Welsh that stuck in my eye – the bit about God so loving the world he gave it his only son. The clock swivels its hands to cover its eyes.

Verb – to glorify.

A row of children clapping their hands. Delighted children watching cartoons, kids with no mams or dads. Louise told me about the people-smugglers and the syrup they gave the children. They made them drink it. She stood on the beach at Kos and welcomed the children into Europe.

On my TV, the news reporter holds the microphone up to the little girl.

Would you like any painkillers? Do you need any help? Sit up, I'll do your pillows. A mug of hot chocolate. The simple things in life.

Louise said to be a poet you had to be an active witness in the world.

A future to believe in.

Pretty flamingo. Tucked my toothbrush into my waistband and got on my crutches, headed to the bathroom.

The sound of vomiting and running feet. Oh, it's brown. I feel guilty for that... I feel awful now.

Dignity.

To glorify – extol.

She is 87-years-old.

I just heard the nurse say.

*

Cherry juice running down my chin and this morning's papers, this thin blue line and the fragments of a night time scene... a voice from Eastern Europe: do not get out of bed lady, I am telling you five times already... I cannot clean you properly if you do not stay still... I know it hurts, yes I know, I need you to be brave and stop shouting...

The days in here are slowing down, emulsifying. Your blood pressure has gone down nicely, she said. Dreamt I was searching an indoor market for a smart pair of shoes, there was a pair of powder blue loafers and some dark brogues, looked like snakeskin or crocodile...

... something relating to the ankle, a pin in there tomorrow, we can rebuild him, written to stay awake until the night properly kicks in with full exhaustion...

Mobile phone calls, tweets. An article about Stuart George and Bowie in the paper, all this inanity plastered across the pages to stop people waking up... these Fragmins I have shored against my ruin... There is a tale to be told about Zambia... people are so fucking fragile, they bruise like flowers unfolding under fluorescent light... my friend came laden with fruit but now it's NIL BY MOUTH...

Today is Thursday.

They're putting me to sleep soon.

I hope I wake up

The Last Of The Redskins

– Should ban that bastard Fair from this town!

Rawlings bangs his pipe on the dashboard, showering Phil's leg with sparks and smouldering bits of twisted black debris. Phil brushes it off and winds down the passenger side window an inch. It's battering down with rain outside.

– Oh aye, he says, – why's that then?

Rawlings stuffs the bowl full of Samson and tries to fire it up one handed, other hand on the steering wheel as the red-cloaked wagon crawls slowly along Anlaby Road, grinding stop-start forward among the snail-pace procession of traffic.

– Look at - *click* - this - *click* - fuckin - *click, click* - lot, he goes.

Stem clenched between teeth, he clicks and sucks and smacks his lips, but the ripe smelling shag refuses to ignite.

– Bastard thing!

He flings the green clipper into the foot well and beckons across to Phil.

– Gis that fuckin lighter of yours.

Phil hands it over.

– Nowt to do with Fair this, Phil says. – Just normal early morning traffic. Fair's not even open while dinnertime.

– Dunt fuckin help though, does it? Bastard thing!

The tobacco starts to smoulder under the steady flame. Rawlings pulls hard, expelling furious plumes against the water-blurred windscreen, then jams the lighter into the top pocket of his filthy once-green body warmer, oblivious to the expectant hand of his travelling companion.

– And I'll tell yer summat else an' all, he says, – it sucks all the money out o' the town.

He extracts his pipe and points the stem beyond the glass, at the early morning commuters and shoppers huddled damp beneath umbrellas and hoods, or peering from bus shelters that afford temporary sanctuary from the bouncing rain.

– These daft cunts, they'd rather spend it all on fuckin balloons and dodgem rides than feed their bastard families. Make me fuckin badly, they do. And then, after this lot's fucked off, you know what's next on the shopping list, don't yer?

– No, what?

– Fireworks! Fuckin crackers and bangers and bastard sparklers! Firing all their wages up into the fuckin sky!

Here we go, thinks Phil. Not even got the rope off yet and the mad old bastard's off on one.

– Not going to Fair this year then, Jeff?

–You what? Rawlings's face contorts with disgust. – I'd rather put me cock in a fuckin blender. Hull fuckin Fair? They should be made to queue for bread, like they do in bastard Russia.

– I think it's mint, Phil tells him

– Mint? *Mint?* Rawlings coughs the word up like it's an actual mint that's got stuck down his throat. – What's fuckin *mint* about it? The pipe jumps up and down in his red flushed face, sends more sparks bouncing off the back of white-knuckled hands that grip the wheel. Phil imagines his employer strapped against his will into some death-defying fairground ride, howling with rage as he's launched into the sky at one hundred miles an hour, a tornado of burning banknotes spiralling around him. He lifts his newspaper to conceal the grin that unfolds across his face.

– It's a good job it's only taties we've got on the back, Phil says, – and not sticks of dynamite, else we'd have both been blown sky high before we'd got five yards up the road.

Rawlings just grunts and sucks on his pipe. Some mornings you don't get two words out of him, but Phil can tell today's gonna be a pearler. The old man's chomping at the stem and growling under his breath at the surrounding traffic, half of which has probably not got tax discs or proper insurance, or they're definitely being driven as getaway cars by murdering Kosovans or single mothers who got them off the dole along with their free nappies and free curtains and free Lambert and Butler.

Phil scours the paper for some proper bait to throw. Fish when the fish are biting. Surely the Super Soar Away Sun can deliver some suitable ammunition before they get to Harold's for the first drop? Phil flicks through the various headlines: soldier's limbs mangled by landmines... drunken celebrity flesh flashed from the back of limousines... footballers fighting in nightclubs... politicians caught with their hands in public purses... the usual tabloid shite. But nothing that would properly light

172

the blue touch paper smouldering to his right. Phil decides outright lies and invention to be the best option.

He slaps the paper.

– Fuckin marvellous, innit. Bloke here, been in Hull ten minutes and he's been given a grant by the City of Culture to start up an Albanian Juggling Circus Show.

Snort of derision from the driver's seat. Thump of briar on dashboard.

– Nowt surprises me with this fuckin council. Surprised they ant given the cunt the keys to the bastard city.

*

They turn off Anlaby Road and pass the row of shops that serve the top end of Hawthorn Avenue. Rawlings swings the wheel over to the kerb and slams on the brakes.

He points across the road.

– Light on in that fish shop, he says.

And there is, a dim yellow glow through the newspapers pasted across the glass frontage. The Silver Net; once more occupied, its former owner – Alvin McKenzie – having vacated the premises some six months previous, pursued by various outstanding debts. Gambling, some people reckoned. The woman in the nearby newsagent where Phil sometimes buys cigarettes and chocolate painted a more lurid picture; burly shaven-headed men in designer sportswear arriving in blacked out 4x4s, banging on doors and rattling windows in the dead of night. Drug dealers, she reckoned. Drug dealers from out of town. Liverpool, she said. Phil wasn't convinced. Most casual gossip in the area was founded on varying degrees of suspicion, idle mischief-making and outright fantasy. Alvin didn't seem the type to be involved in drugs, either the consumption or retail thereof. His only visible vice was a flutter on the gee-gees and the most exotic substance available at The Silver Net was a Spam Fritter and Chips Dinnertime Special at £1.99, with a choice of curry, gravy or mushy peas in a tray, breadcake included.

Rawlings had taken a more pragmatic view. Regardless of local conjecture, the only account he was interested in was the one Alvin had left outstanding for three ton of Pentland Javelin, stacked up over a period of weeks in the shed round the back of the shop. Phil could bear personal witness to this particular debt; he was the one who had done all the stacking.

Rawlings bangs on the fish shop front until a sandy-haired kid of about sixteen or so emerges from the back and sticks his skinny freckled face around the door.

– A'right?

Rawlings tips his hat. – Any taties? he says.

As a Rawlings Potato Merchants employee of three years standing, Phil recognises this opening gambit as more a challenge than an offer. To those unfamiliar with his business methods, what Rawlings actually means is 'How many taties are you having off me and how soon can you pay me?'

The lad's eyes widen and his Adam's apple jerks up and down in his throat.

– Ah cuh-cuh-cuh-uh, er... ah cuh-cuh...

Rawlings regards him impassively from behind a steady billowing of blue smoke.

– Ah cuh-cuh-cuh... CUH-CUH...

A sigh from Rawlings.

– Yeah, alright. Is your father in?

174

– Ah… yeh…

The lad ducks his head back inside and is replaced ten seconds later by an older man wiping his hands on a tea towel, eyebrows raised in enquiry.

– Yes, hello, good morning now, says Rawlings. – I supplied Alvin.

He jerks his thumb over at the wagon.

– Got Cara on the back. Redskins.

– Ah da-da-da-da-da-da-uuuuuh-huh…

The man coughs, swallows hard and tries again:

– Don't – tah… DON'T *NNNNNNEED* UM YET…

– Oh, for fucks sake, says Rawlings. – Not another stuttering cunt.

And he turns on his heel and strides off back to the wagon, leaving Phil and the new proprietor stood staring at each other in dumb disbelief. Phil shrugs, turns and trots off after his glorious leader. He climbs back up into the already gunning cab, which lurches off up Hawthorn Ave and out onto Hessle Road.

– That was a bit much, Phil says.

– What was?

– Talking to that bloke like that. He can't help it if he's got a speech defect.

– Well, I'm sorry, says Rawlings, – but I ant got all morning. Anyway, you can't do business with people like that.

– People like what?

– The handicapped.

Phil laughs and shakes his head in disbelief.

– He's not fuckin handicapped!

– Well, what is he then?

Phil doesn't answer. Then he says, – You should have asked him where Alvin's gone.

Rawlings considers this for a beat, but then shakes his head.

– Be there all fuckin day.

But Phil can almost see the notion spinning round underneath Rawlings's hat, a tweed affair with a little feather perched on the side. Probably a smart hat once, but now long ruined; trampled on by mud-encrusted boots, dropped in warehouses, blown off into puddles by the wind, dragged across fields, rolled on and/or chewed by dogs, pigs, horses etc, singed with hot tobacco smoke, spattered with engine oil and chip fat – forty-five long back-breaking hard-working sweat-streaked years at the cutting edge of The Tatie Game, which, as Rawlings will grimly inform you, is The Hardest Game There Is, especially today, oh aye, yes indeed boyo, what with The Fucking EU and The Fucking Government and Pound Shops and Car Boot Sales and Supermarkets and Immigrants and Fucking Benefit Cheats and People On Diets or People On Council Estates or just People In General, not to mention The City Of Bastard Culture and Firework Night and Hull Bastard Fair.

– Nah, bollocks to it, says Rawlings. – Alvin's long gone. Probably at the bottom of King George Dock. Won't see him again. Or my bastard money.

*

By the time Rawlings parks up outside Crawley's Fruit & Veg, the rain has slowed to a weak drizzle. Phil unties the sheet, rolling it back to reveal the rear of the wagon. Twelve bags of redskins handballed into the store-room at the back of the shop. The first couple of drops are always the hardest, Phil swaying beneath each twenty-five kilo sack, bumping hips and scraping knuckles off side passage walls and rough wooden pallets as last night's lager slowly seeps out of his system. Phil staggers to and from the wagon while Rawlings talks shop with Harold. The taties stack up and the kettle rumbles into life. When the last sack of spuds is laid, the brews are poured and the three men fire up their smokes.

– JOB'S TIGHT, HAROLD, announces Rawlings. – TIGHTER THAN A NUN'S CUNT.

Harold Crawley's ancient face creases into a sad rheumy-eyed smile and he nods yes. Harold is eighty-odd-years-old, an ancient collection of bones shrink-wrapped in yellow parchment. A tiny paper doll of a man. Every morning they bang on his back door and every morning Phil peers through the letter box, half-expecting to see a pair of upturned slippers on the hallway floor. But every morning a frail voice bids their patience as bolts are pulled back by trembling hands, the key is rattled and turned and then the kettle switched on. First drop of the day; strong cups of tea and frozen breath hanging in the small white-washed store-room that smells of damp dogs, Calor Gas and boxes of citrus fruit.

Harold adjusts his hearing aid. A high-pitched whistle causes Phil to wince and the dozing Yorkshire Terrier in the corner to jerk her head up from her blanket. She looks at the three men, yaps once in retort and then curls back to sleep again.

– OH AYE, says Rawlings, – GERRIN HARDER, THIS LARK. MIGHT HAVE TO TURN TO CRIME. HOW YOU FINDING IT THEN, HAROLD? SLOW?

Harold nods and opens his mouth to reply, but before the elderly fruit and veg vendor can utter a word,

Rawlings is bellowing at him again, as though addressing him from the other end of a trawler in high wind.

– YOU KNOW WHAT'S FUCKED THIS JOB UP DON'T YER, HAROLD?

– Supermarkets, murmurs Harold.

– BASTARD SUPERMARKETS, THAT'S WHAT! THAT FUCKIN ASDA! CAN GET OWT IN THERE NOW. PAY YER GAS BILL, GET YER PRESCRIPTION, SORT OUT YER CAR INSURANCE. EVEN BE ABLE TO *BUY* A FUCKIN CAR IN A SUPERMARKET SOON. OH AYE, WRITING'S ON THE WALL, YOU MARK MY WORDS, BOYO!

– Ey Jeff, says Harold, – d'yer know anyone who's got an 'oss?

– AN 'OSS? WHY, YER THINKING OF ENTERING THE GRAND NATIONAL?

A phone starts ringing somewhere, another room. Phil looks down the hallway into the kitchen and sees Harold's eldest son Arthur seated at the table, picking at a plate of bacon and eggs, the telephone jangling at his elbow.

– Nah, it's not for me, says Harold, – it's for our lass. She's got a wart on her arse and I was wanting an 'oss 'air, y'know, ter tek it off like.

– YOUR LASS? WHAT LASS? DON'T TELL ME YER COURTING, HAROLD!?

The phone rings and rings and rings. Arthur sets his knife and fork down, pushes his plate away and unfurls the morning paper.

– Oh aye, nods Harold. – Met her down the Britannia. Smashing lass. But this wart's giving her right jip. Can't set hersen down proper.

Still the insistent clamour of the phone. Still Arthur is oblivious.

Phil taps Harold on the shoulder

178

– Harold, he says, – phone.

Harold smiles and nods. Phil lifts his fist to the side of his face, thumb to his ear, his little finger at his mouth, points down the hallway.

– PHONE, he says.

– Oh, righto...

Harold sets off down the hallway for the kitchen, slippered feet shuffling on lino, one hand on the wall for support.

Rawlings produces a notebook and pencil from his top pocket, starts scribbling Harold's chit.

– How many was it? A dozen?

– Yeah, says Phil.

Rawlings licks the end of his pencil, makes deft strokes, tears off the chit and pins it up on the cork notice board above the sink. Phil gulps down the dregs of his tea, sets his mug down on the side and glances back down the hallway. He gauges it to be roughly thirty feet long and Harold is about a quarter of the way down. For every peal of the phone, Harold is taking half a step, pausing every two steps to lean against the wall and regain his breath.

Jesus, thinks Phil. If there's ever a fire in here then he's proper fucked.

Eventually, Harold reaches the kitchen table. He picks up the receiver from its cradle and says hello, listens. Then he hands it to Arthur.

– It's for you, he says.

Phil and Rawlings look at each other. Rawlings shakes his head.

– Unbelievable, he says. – Fuckin unbelievable.

He bangs his pipe against the wall, showers the stone floor with smouldering fragments and grinds them underfoot till the sparks are black smears.

– C'mon, he says, – let's get shifted.

*

They park up opposite Tooty Fruity on Hessle Road. Rawlings takes a long steaming piss against the side of the wagon, the dark pool spreading slowly between his battered old brogues and rolling away down a kerbside drain. He nods across to the stack of brown and red sacks on the shop front that Phil had built three days previous.

– Count up how many he's got left there, says Rawlings.

– Fifteen or so, says Phil.

Rawlings shakes and packs away his tackle. Hitches up his breeches and fastens his belt.

– Get one off the back and tek it in, open it up for him. I'm gunna go in that shop and get a few lighters.

Rawlings disappears into a nearby newsagent as Phil shoulders a sack of redskins and crosses the road.

The young lass in Tooty Fruity's is at the scales with a customer.

– Be with you in one minute, she says, dropping carrots into a paper bag.

The customer glances round at Phil's entry. His smile of acknowledgment suddenly switches to one of recognition.

– Oh, hello, he says.

For a second or so, Phil's mind is a complete blank. The man has a vaguely familiar face, but Phil struggles to place him. Late forties, balding. Mournful-looking bloke. Dark rings under tired-looking eyes that slide up and down Phil in a vaguely accusatory manner, from work boots to tatty old mud-spattered jacket to the baseball cap on his head and the twenty-five kilo sack of spuds slumped over his right shoulder.

Then Phil's brain suddenly clicks into gear and he sees the man sat behind a desk with a pen in his hand and a blue and white badge on his shirt.

Oh fucking marvellous, thinks Phil. It's the bloke who signs me on.

– Alright mate, says Phil.

He turns to the lass at the scales and slaps the sack on his shoulder.

– Just these please, love. Fiver, innit?

– You what?

– Five quid? I think that's what the sign outside said... here y'are...

He digs a handful of coins out of his jeans pocket and counts them out one-handed onto the counter.

– ... three... four... four-fifty... a fiver. Alright? Cheers then love, ta-ra.

Phil gives the bloke a curt nod, swivels round and quicksteps out of the shop, onto the street and straight past Rawlings who emerges from the newsagents.

– Quick, get back in, says Phil.

– Ey? Why? What's up?

– Dole!

Phil drags his boss back into the shop and behind the greeting cards and, thus concealed, they survey the street outside from behind verses of congratulation and commiseration until Dole Man and his bag of best English carrots have left Tooty Fruity and are safely out of sight.

*

After two more fruit shops and a fish shop they head to Spring Bank to see Druggy Bob at Plants International. The front of the shop is empty of customers, the radio playing to buckets of fresh flowers, boxes of fruit and shelves thick with greenery. Phil shouts hello and they wander through to the kitchen and out to the back yard.

Druggy Bob is stood gazing thoughtfully into the open doorway of the small garage that serves as a storeroom.

– Alright Bob, says Phil.

Bob looks round, gives them a double-take and then a smile and nod of delayed acknowledgement. His eyes are glassed over, his movements slow and languid with an almost visible air of detached calm. Stoned, thinks Phil.

– Do you know any decent builders? Bob says.

– Builders? repeats Rawlings. – What you want a builder for?

Druggy Bob points into his garage.

– I'm thinking of having this made into a flat.

– A flat? says Phil. – How can that be a flat? Who's gunna live in that?

– Bed-sit then. Perfect for a single person. Student, summat like that.

Phil leans past Bob and peers into the gloom. He sees crates of junk, pallets stacked with sacks, sheets of tarpaulin, drums of vegetable oil, rusting metal buckets half full of greasy water, tins of long-hardened emulsion, stiffened paint brushes, yard brushes, spades, shovels, hoes, trowels, engine parts, coils of old rope, a partly dismantled motorbike propped up at the far end under an ancient dart board.

– What about all that shit?

– Just shift it all up one end. Put a wall in.

Phil withdraws his head and shakes it in the negative.

– Are you tekkin the piss? You can't turn that into a flat!

Bob frowns, genuinely mystified.

– Why can't I? he asks.

– Why? It's a concrete fuckin box, Bob!

– So what? That's what flats are made of aren't they? What's yours made of, cardboard?

– Bob, no cunt would live in that.

– Get an Asylum Seeker in there.

– How the fuck they gunna breathe? There's no windows!

– Well, they'd be used to that wunt they. All come over in the back of lorries, don't they?

Phil gives him a look, incredulous. Bob shrugs.

– They could leave the door open, he says.

Rawlings, tired of this debate, asks Bob how many taties he wants.

Bob picks up a blackened potato and slings it to the far end of the garage. It bounces off the half-stacked pallet in the corner and splatters against the wall.

– Still got ten bags there from last week. Just give us five.

– Five? says Rawlings. – Come on Rigsby, you'll need more than that just to feed yer new tenants.

Bob smiles and then claps his hand to his forehead as if struck by a sudden illumination.

– Hey Jeff! he says, – you like classical music, don't yer?

– Can't abide it, says Rawlings.

– Ere y'are, says Bob, – come an' have a look at these…

They follow Druggy Bob back through into the kitchen. He roots around in the cupboard beneath the sink and pulls out various DVD cases. He fans them out for inspection like a hand of oversized playing cards. The covers feature the busts of classical composers, stern faces carved in white stone against a dark blue background, ornate gold italics above: *The Complete Classical Collection.*

– Drop us another five bags in and I'll gi'yer these.

– What the fuck would I want with them? says Rawlings.

– Worth about hundred and twenty quid on eBay, these.

Rawlings turns to Phil. – Have I got fuckin mug written across my forehead in big bastard letters? Have I?

– Nah, look, protests Bob, – it's got the lot on here: Mozart, Chopin, Tchaikovsky, that deaf German cunt, the whole fuckin gang of 'em. Twenty CDs. It's the complete collection.

He hands one of the cases across to Phil who examines the cover and then turns it over to study the track details on the back. Phil hands it back.

– Not my thing, ta, Bob. Got any reggae? Bob Marley, owt like that?

– No, but I've got songs from the shows. Hang on a minute...

Druggy Bob delves under the sink again and starts pulling out various artefacts: torches, screwdriver sets, CDs, DVDs, hardback books, boxes of chocolates.

Rawlings rolls his eyes, starts filling his pipe.

– Start bringing 'em in, he says to Phil, – or else we'll be here all bastard day.

Outside, the rain has finally stopped. Phil strips the cover off the wagon, rolls it up on the pavement and jams it underneath the front pallets. When he gets back in with the first sack on his shoulder, Bob has what looks like half of HMV spread out on the kitchen table. Rawlings leans over the selection and points with the stem of his pipe.

– Right, I'll have this one, Lullaby of Broadway, The Three Tenors and them classical ones.

He turns to Phil. – A dozen in the back, he tells him.

– Aye aye, skipper, says Phil.

Phil stacks the potatoes in the soon-to-be luxury playboy apartment and then joins Rawlings in the wagon. He makes a show of checking all his pockets, patting the front of his jacket and jeans.

– Hang on a sec, he says. – Dropped me tabs.

Then he ducks back into Bob's and gets a quarter of weed, a wrap of MDMA and the promise of *Legend – The Best of Bob Marley* by this time next week.

*

Young Fletcher's head darts out of the side door as the wagon pulls up next to Fletchers. He seems agitated, even more so than usual. Phil can see him in the wing mirror, leaping up and down and waving his arms about, like he's directing a plane in for landing.

– WHOA! he goes, – WHOA WHOA WHOA!

He jogs round to the driver's side and pulls himself up on the foot rail. An irate face pops into view as Rawlings winds the window down.

– Jeff! What you doing?

Rawlings squints down at Young Fletcher through a freshly exhaled swathe of Samson.

– What am I doing? I'm trying to earn a living, what's it look like?

– I don't want you today, says Young Fletcher. He coughs, grimaces, fans the smoke away with his hand. – Fucking hell, that stinks, he says.

– What you mean you don't want me today? says Rawlings

– Next Friday I said!

– You said a ton today!

Young Fletcher shakes his head firmly in the negative. – I dint say that. No way. When did I say that?

– Last time I was here! A ton next Friday, you said.

Rawlings turns to Phil. – Did he say or did he not say to come with a load this Friday? Last time we was here? Did he or did he not say that?

– Don't fuckin involve me, says Phil.

– Next Friday! yells Young Fletcher. – I said *next* Friday, not *this* Friday

– It's next Friday now.

– No it int!

– Well fuck me, how many Fridays has there been between then and now?

– How the fuck can it be next Friday? It's this Friday! You was here last Monday and I said come next Friday, I dint say come *this* Friday. I said *next* Friday.

Rawlings sighs, pushes his hat to the back of his head and runs a hand through his thick ginger hair. Pulls his pipe out and bangs it on the dashboard. Looks across at Phil.

– See what I have to put up with? Dunt even know the days of the fuckin week, this soft cunt.

Young Fletcher sighs and rolls his eyes. It occurs to Phil, from his passenger position, that Young Fletcher looks like a talking head on a TV screen, a politician resolutely disagreeing with a moot point posed by a dogged interviewer in front of a live studio audience. Constant rebuttal as the first form of defence.

– I don't want owt dropping today Jeff, he says. – Can't move for fuckin taties in there!

Rawlings kills the engine and shoves open the cab door, causing Young Fletcher to let go and spring backwards. He twists in mid-air and stumbles into the wheelie bins as he lands, nearly knocking them over.

– EY! he shrieks, – MIND WHAT YER DOING!

– Oh, shut up you big fuckin tart, says Rawlings, jumping down from the wagon. – Gerrin there and mek us two of them big bacon banjos. And get that kettle on.

The two potato delivery men enter the shop, go through to the back and install themselves around the staff room table alongside Karen and Brenda, two of the women from the shop, on their tea break. The sandwiches are eventually brought by a grumbling Young Fletcher, who then informs Rawlings in no uncertain terms to stay there and not bother him while he gets on with sorting out last month's staff hours. Rawlings replies that he hopes Young Fletcher has a calendar handy so he can tell one day from the fuckin next. Phil chuckles and flicks the kettle on.

– Now then, Jeff, says Brenda.

Rawlings nods how do and unwraps his sandwich. He stuffs it into his mouth and tears off half in one go. He flips open a *Daily Mirror* to the racing page.

The younger lass, Karen, is showing Brenda a succession of photographs on a mobile phone. Phil remembers that Karen's been off work the last few weeks on maternity leave. He tries to remember what she looked like when she was pregnant; tries to picture her with that yellow tabard stretched taut across a huge swollen stomach. The girl sat opposite him is as narrow as a toothpick. She leans into the older woman and clicks through the images one by one.

– That's him in his Moses basket, look...

– Ah, says Brenda, – int he bonny!

– ... and that's him in the bath with his Iggle Piggle... our Ronnie got him that...

– Bless!

– Oh, he won't go anywhere without his Iggle Piggle... and that's him asleep with his Nana...

– Is that your mam, Karen?

– No, that's Steve's mam... hang on... that's my mam, look... and look, that's him watching telly, look...

– He's beautiful, Karen, absolutely gorgeous!

Brenda nudges Rawlings.

– Here Jeff, have a look. Karen's little 'un. Show Jeff, Karen.

– Karen thrusts the phone past Brenda and into the space between Rawlings's nose and the *Daily Mirror*. He barely glances at it before his eyes shoot back to the racing page.

– Aye, yes, very nice, he says.

– There's a better one of him here somewhere, says Karen, oblivious to the older man's obvious disinterest. – Hang on... oh, no, not that one... there's one with his eyes open somewhere... hang on...

– Yes, alright love, you can take them away now, thank you, says Rawlings.

– Ooh, he's an ignorant bleeder int he, him, Brenda says.

– I've had all my babies thank you very much, announces Rawlings, eyes still locked on the 2.30 card for Lingford. – I don't need to see any more.

Brenda looks at Phil, who grins and shrugs.

– How the 'ell do you put up with him all day? she says.

– Ere y'are Karen, says Phil, – let's have a look. He leans across the table towards the younger woman, who proffers the phone and resumes her running commentary.

– That's him with his cousin... that's our Sharon's bain, Cameron... an' that's him with our Sharon...

Rawlings slings the paper back onto the table, picks up the remnants of his bacon banjo and folds it into his mouth. He chews, swallows, then drains his mug of tea with a theatrical smack of the lips. Belches, frowns, pokes around in his mouth with stained brown fingers and pulls a string of bacon fat from between his teeth. He examines it and flicks it towards the bin in the corner.

Brenda stares at him with barely concealed disgust.

– Is there any need? she says.

Rawlings wipes his hands on his body warmer and rises, signalling for Phil to finish his drink.

– Come on you, finish that drop. We're off.

Phil takes a tentative sip of his tea. It's still piping hot. He slides his mug to the centre of the table, scoops up his sandwich and gets to his feet

– Ta-ra, Brenda, he says.

– Ta-ra, Phil, says Brenda.

– Ta-ra, Karen. She's lovely.

– It's a *he*, says Karen.

– He, sorry, says Phil, and he follows Rawlings out the door.

They pass Young Fletcher in the back way. He's sat at a small desk staring at a spreadsheet on a computer screen, an open cash box overflowing with scraps of paper and receipts. He silently mouths numbers as he taps the keyboard. Rawlings slaps him on the back as he passes.

– We're away, he says.

Phil stops at the desk, lowers his face next to Young Fletcher's and whispers, – Thirty-three... two thousand and four... eight hundred and seventy-two...

Young Fletcher flaps his hand angrily, as though batting away a wasp.

– Next Friday, says Rawlings.

– Yeah, whatever, says Young Fletcher.

They climb up into the cab and Rawlings starts the engine. He notices Phil looking at him.

– What's up with your face? he says.

– You, says Phil.

– What?

– You could have at least looked at her photos.

– What do I want to be looking at bains for? All look the bastard same anyway, when they're that age.

As they're pulling away from the kerb they hear a voice yelling at them to stop. Phil looks in the wing mirror and sees Young Fletcher hanging out of the side door.

– OI! shouts Young Fletcher. – YOU DIN'T PAY ME FOR THEM SANDWICHES!

– I think he wants you to stop, Phil says.

Rawlings swivels his eyes across to the wing mirror and then back to the road.

– I'll see him next Friday, he says.

*

– This has fucked me right up, this has.

Rawlings guns the wagon along Cottingham Road, his agitation measured out in short noxious blasts of his pipe.

The previous three drops had been swift in-and-out jobs, each one of them resolutely refusing to be up-sold. Worthington's on Beverley Road only took their usual twenty, Eric Clough at The Rose Bowl didn't have room for any extra and Glenda on Newland agreed to take a half dozen more before promptly changing her mind after Rawlings had criticised her Halloween Pumpkin display. Even the normally affable Mr Chan at The Golden Dragon had refused to squeeze a few extra into his shed.

A ton of surplus redskins and no ready takers.

– Put yer fuckin thinking cap on boyo, says Rawlings.

Phil tries to think of someone on the round who Rawlings hadn't offended in the last three months.

– What about Barbara on Orchard? he says. – We ant been there for ages.

– That's because I told her husband to fuck off.

– Did yer? When?

– Couple of weeks ago.

– Why'd'yer do that?

– Coz he was being a cunt.

Phil considers the probability of this and nods assent. Then a fresh possibility occurs.

– Ey, warrabout Hardakers? Up at Beverley? He's got a big fuck-off warehouse.

The wagon stops at a red light. Phil watches a group of students cross in front of them, three girls and a lad wearing a dark purple hoodie emblazoned with HULL UNIVERSITY CANOE CLUB in bright yellow. They are carrying books and folders and bags. One of the girls drops a black folder, which bursts open and spills paper out onto the road. They all stop to gather up the sheets as the lights change from red to amber and the traffic starts to roll forward. Rawlings leans on his horn as the students dance in and out of the vehicles and across to the other side, waving handfuls of paper in apology.

– Look at these daft bastards. All that education and they ant got the sense to gerrout the way of a ten-ton truck.

Phil watches the lad kneel down on the pavement and gather the papers together and stuff them back in the girl's folder as the wagon trundles past them.

– I could have gone to University, says Phil.

Rawlings grunts acknowledgement but deems this information worthy of no further comment. He turns the wheel left towards Beverley and steps on the gas as they clear the lights at the top of Cottingham Road.

– Fuck it, he says. – Let's go and see that daft bugger up at Hardakers...

*

Phil switches the radio on as the wagon flies past green fields still damp with the rain of early morning. He fiddles with the dial until he finds Classic FM and the cab is filled with the dark and sombre scrapings of an eighteenth century string quartet. He picks up one of the Classical Collection CD boxes and reads the titles of the compositions.

– What you gunna do with these? he asks Rawlings.

– Christmas present.

– Who for? Someone you don't like?

– The wife's father can have 'em.

– Is he a lover of the classics?

– He is now, says Rawlings.

Phil tosses the box back into the glove compartment, lights a tab and stares out of the passenger window.

Hardakers was an inspired suggestion, he thinks. Bollocks to driving round Hull all day trying to find a home for a spare ton of redskins. This way, it's one more drop and then straight back to the flat. Be home for half two at the latest. Roll himself a big spliff and mong out in front of afternoon telly. *Jeremy Kyle, Judge Judy, Cash In The Attic*. Marvellous. He pats the bag of weed that nestles in his top pocket. That last quarter he got off Bob was top drawer. He hopes this is the same gear. A few joints, a few tinnies, and then a line or two of Magic to launch himself round town and into the weekend. Phil's Friday ritual.

– Some of the shite he has in that back way, says Rawlings, – I don't know why he just dunt shut up shop and do the car boots, have done with it. Make more money than he does flogging fucking flowers, I know that.

– Who? says Phil.

– Bob. Druggy fuckin Bob.

– Them out of date Belgian biscuits he had were nice. Remember them?

A grimace from Rawlings. – Beats me how he stays in business. Off his bloody head all the time.

– Who? Bob? D'yer reckon?

– Do I reckon?! You look at his eyes next time we're there. Like looking into the eyes of a goat.

Phil laughs. – Fuck you on about, a goat?

– You look into a goat's eyes, next time you see one. Dead, they are. All glazed over. That's what Bob's eyes are like. Pumped full o' drugs. You have a look, next time we're there.

– And when am I likely to come across a goat? says Phil.

Rawlings shakes his head grimly. – Anyone caught for drugs, instant death penalty.

– You serious? Capital punishment for dealing drugs?

– Dealing 'em, tekking 'em, having owt to do with 'em.

Rawlings leans down and slams the dashboard with the palm of his hand. – Caught for drugs: instant death penalty. No fuckin about.

– What type of drugs?

– Any type. All of 'em.

– What, even like... Lemsip?

– You know what I'm on about. All that dope and heroin and that.

Phil considers this. – How would you kill 'em?

– Lethal injection. Humane. Or else gi'em one o' them cocktails.

– What, like Sex On The Beach?

– No, like one o' them they gi'yer in the hospital. Don't know what they're called. Red and green tablet they gi'yer.

– What you on about?

– That cocktail they hand out in hospital to sup yer off.

Phil laughs. – You don't half come out with some shit, Jeff.

– Oh, yer think so d'yer? Seen it meself, boyo. When our Norman was in that cancer ward.

– Norman? Your brother?

Rawlings nods. – Screaming his heart out with the pain, he was. Riddled with it, he was. The only thing in his body that didn't hurt was his tongue, and that was only coz it dint have a bone in it.

– Jesus, says Phil.

– Oh, heart-breaking it was. Heart-breaking. In the end, I went and got the nurse and said ey look, c'mon, this is out of fuckin order, this. Surely there must be summat you can give him, I said.

Rawlings coughs, takes his pipe from his mouth and bangs the briar hard, once, twice, and then lays it out on the dashboard. Pulls his baccie pouch from his pocket and opens it out on his knee.

– Anyroad, she went off and came back with this doctor. They asked me if I was absolutely certain that I wanted it stopping, as his next of kin, like. And I said aye, go on, gerron with it. Couldn't carry on like that. Screaming like a stuck pig, he was.

He takes a big pinch of Samson and stuffs the bowl of the pipe one-handed, packing it in tight with his thumb. Puts the pipe back down carefully onto the dashboard and rummages into the depths of his body warmer.

– Five bastard lighters I bought. Ere y'are, take this...

Phil leans across and holds the steering wheel steady as Rawlings scours all of his pockets with both hands, pulling out old receipts, lottery tickets, betting shop pens and handfuls of copper, cursing and muttering until he finally raises himself slightly off the seat and locates a plastic yellow lighter in the depths of his trouser arse-pocket. He retrieves his pipe and holds the flame to the bowl until it glows red.

– Ta, he says, and takes back the wheel.

Rawlings sucks greedily on the stem and exhales a stream of smoke out of the half open window. Phil is about to say something, but then the older man continues:

– So anyway, they pulled the curtain round and give him these two tablets. A green 'un and a red 'un. Fifteen minutes later he was gone.

– Dead?

– I fuckin hope so, says Rawlings. – We buried him.

Phil contemplates this for a minute or so. He becomes conscious of his tongue in his mouth, the space it occupies. He runs it along the top row of his teeth. Tries to imagine what such pain must feel like.

– Fuck me, he says finally, – that's horrible.

Rawlings shakes his head. – Merciful is what it was.

He moves down the gears and turns the wagon off the dual carriageway, down the side road and past the mud-spattered sign:

HARDAKER'S GARDEN AND GOLF CENTRE – "PARADISE FOUND"

*

Steve Hardaker agrees to take the last of the redskins and hands over the big bunch of keys for the warehouse and the small key for the forklift. Rawlings backs the wagon down the long dirt track behind the main Garden Centre and into the fields that house both the warehouse and the driving range. Once the wagon is positioned in front of the warehouse doors, Rawlings kills the engine, climbs down from the cab, relights his pipe and saunters back up towards the Garden Centre.

– Sort that lot out, he says to Phil. – I'll go and have a word with soppy bollocks.

Phil pulls himself up onto the back of the wagon and re-arranges the remaining sacks of spuds onto a nearside pallet. Then he jumps down to unlock and swing open the large double-doors to the warehouse.

The forklift splutters into life on the fourth twist of the key. Phil raises the forks as he approaches the side of the wagon, spears and lifts the pallet, then retreats slowly and carefully into the shadows of the warehouse. He lowers the pallet and executes a deft three-hundred-and-sixty-

196

degree turn, scoots over to the furthest darkest corner, sets the load down safely and then spins the forklift back round to rest in its original position in the middle of the warehouse. He turns off the motor but remains in the seat to roll a spliff. He jams it into his mouth, hops off the forklift and wanders back out into the pale October sunlight.

There's a few golf balls left scattered around on the driving range. Phil picks one up, feels its weight in his hand and then leans back, hurls it upward. He shields his eyes to watch it rise, rise, rise and hang in the sky, a tiny black spot against the sun. He rubs his fist into his face, then squats down and gathers up a half dozen or so more golf balls. He straightens up and, with his eyes screwed tight, launches the balls as hard and as high as he can, one after the other into the imagined distance.

He wanders back to the warehouse and sits up on the back of the wagon, sparks his smoke. He fishes his mobile out from his pocket and then remembers that it's dead; no credit left. He tries to work out what time it is by the position of the sun in the sky. He reckons it to be about one, half one.

Phil remembers one time at the back end of last summer when he knocked off work in the early afternoon and went straight on the piss with a few of the lads. After several pints and countless joints and endless games of killer, he went back to the flat at tea-time to crash and burn. He woke up on the couch still in all his work gear, mouth an ashtray, head still banging with booze. The clock on the wall had said twenty past seven and he'd bolted out the door in a blind panic, knowing that Rawlings was due to pick him up at the top of the road at half past on the dot. He remembers the sky was just starting to get light, although the yellow streetlamps were still on. There seemed to be more traffic than usual for that time of the morning, more people on the streets.

It was only when he went for his morning paper and saw the CLOSED sign in the newsagents and caught the whiff of heat and vinegar from the chip shop next door, open and serving, that it started to dawn on him. His vague recognition of events was confirmed when he saw his cousin Deano and their lass crossing the road over to him, all togged up in their best going out gear.

That's when the penny dropped – it was half past seven in the evening. He'd only been asleep a few hours, but had slept so hard and so heavy that he thought it was the next morning. That strange half-light of the fading summer, when twilight could pass for the start of the day.

Phil finishes his spliff and grinds the butt to shreds under his heel on the back of the wagon. Then he stacks the remaining pallets up into two piles of four and lashes them down with a length of oily rope. He wipes his hands on his jeans and sits with his back against the wooden stack, waiting for the older man to return.

*

The Silver Net. The newspapers are down, the windows are steamed and the front door is open.

– C'mon, says Rawlings, – let's see what Wobble Gob's go to say about my money.

The young freckle-faced lad and his father are both stood behind the range. The place smells of disinfectant and cooking fat. Father and son look up, and the father's smile of greeting freezes in a grimace.

– Ah t-t-t-t-told yer...

Rawlings holds his hands up in appeal.

– I'm not here to sell, I was wanting to ask yer about Alvin.

– Who?

– Bloke who had this place, 'bout six month back. Owes me for taties.

The man shakes his head.

– He's d-d-d-d-d...

Phil finds himself involuntarily rising up on the balls of his feet, almost up on his tiptoes, straining forward with each syllable.

– ... d-d-d-d-d-d-d-d...

– Dead? says Phil

The father nods.

– Dead, aye.

Phil glances at Rawlings, but the older man's face does not flicker.

– How?

The father thumps his chest.

– Ah-ah-ah... Heart attack.

– Jesus, says Phil.

– S-s-s-s-stress, says the father.

Rawlings sighs, takes his hat off, rubs a grimy hand through his hair.

– I know how he feels, he says.

Rawlings casts a critical eye around the shop, at the gleaming stainless-steel range, the empty glass fronted hot-box and the pristine white-tiled walls with their recurring blue anchor and net motif. Phil tries to remember what it had looked like when Alvin was there, but struggles to recall any particular details. He seems to remember it as somewhat faded and grubby, ancient gingham curtains, a cracked dirty floor, grease-smeared glass. But perhaps that was only in comparison to how it appears now. The place looks freshly scrubbed, brand new.

– It was up for auction, says the father.

– You've done it out nice, says Rawlings. – New range as well, I see. Needed one, an'all. That one Alvin had was fucked. Always looked like it needed a good scrub. Mind if I have a look?

The father shrugs and stands aside as Rawlings lifts the counter flap and moves behind the range. He lifts a serving ladle and stirs the bubbling fat.

– Gas or electric?

– G-g-g-gas.

– Beef dripping?

– Aye.

Rawlings nods in approval.

– Quickest way to lose money, a chippy. If you don't know what you're doing, like. I've had four o' the bastards. You had a fry on yet?

The father points to a tub of freshly washed and chipped potatoes standing against the back wall. The son scoops up a shovel full and tips them into the fryer. They all lean back as one as the oil hisses, then peer down as the spit and crackle subsides. Rawlings agitates the chips with the ladle, sends them spinning round the fryer like a shoal of angry yellow fish.

– Open for business are we gentlemen?

A Liverpool accent. Two men have entered the shop, two wide set men with shaven heads and heavy jackets buttoned up to the neck. The taller man smiles, but his eyes aren't joining in. His smaller companion takes position in the doorway, arms folded.

Phil takes an instinctive step in retreat, his back up against the range.

– C-c-c-c-c-can I help yer? asks the father.

– Capstone Debt Recovery, says the taller man. – Which one of you gentleman is Mr MacIlroy?

The father coughs twice, clears his throat and says, – Mr Ma-ma-ma-ma-ma...

He stops, wipes his mouth, takes a deep breath and tries again

– He's du-du-du-du

– I'm Mr MacIlroy, says Rawlings.

– Alvin MacIlroy? asks the tall man.

– Yes. What you after?

The man produces a sheet of paper from his pocket, slowly and theatrically unfolds it and holds it up for inspection.

– We are acting on behalf of Davidson Direct Catering who have sold your outstanding debt to Capstone and we are thus authorised to collect payment of the debt in full or goods to the value of the outstanding *FUCK*!

The tall man recoils as if he's been suddenly struck. His hands fly up to his eyes.

– TAKE IT OUT O' THAT YER BASTARD! shouts Rawlings, and Phil sees that he has scooped a ladle full of red hot oil from the fryer and slung it across the range, straight into the tall man's face.

– FUCK! he screams, – ME EYES! ME FUCKIN EYES!

His companion by the door comes forward and Phil leaps out of the way as the ladle flashes up for the second time and the smaller man is spattered in scalding liquid. He yells and then slips on the floor, collapses in a cursing heap, his companion falling on top of him as he stumbles about blindly, clawing frantically at his face.

The taller man is yelling that he can't see, that his eyes are burnt. Rawlings strides round from behind the range and proceeds to batter both of them around the head and shoulders with the ladle, cracking each of their shaven heads in turn.

– GO ON, FUCK OFF OUT OF IT! HARRASSING DECENT WORKING FOLK! BASTARDS! GO ON, FUCK OFF, BEFORE I STICK BOTH YOUR FUCKIN HEADS IN THAT FRYER!

The bailiffs scramble to their feet and get through the door, one of Rawlings's well aimed brogues planted on the arse of the taller man, sending him sprawling once more onto the pavement.

Phil picks up a carving knife from the counter top and follows them out into the street. The two bailiffs get into a black 4x4, the taller man clutching his face and yelling threats from the passenger window.

– YEAH, GO ON YER PAIR OF BASTARDS! yells Phil. – FUCK OFF BEFORE I CARVE YER OPEN!

Rawlings and Phil watch the 4x4 wheel-spin down the street. They're joined by the new proprietor of The Silver Net and his wide-eyed freckle-faced son.

– Have they guh-guh-guh-guh-guh...

– Oh aye, says Rawlings. – And they'll stay gone.

He turns to Phil.

– Come on Phil, he says. – I'll drop you off at home.

*

The cab in motion. Phil stares out of the window at the shop fronts passing by.

– What you doing with yerself rest of the day? asks Rawlings.

– Dunno. Fuck all. Watch telly, I suppose. What you doing?

Rawlings sucks on his pipe and doesn't reply. Then he says, – I'll tell yer summat Phil, if you're clever enough to go to University you should go.

– Nah, too old now.

– Yer never as old as yer will be tomorrow.

– What's that supposed to mean?

Rawlings takes the pipe from his mouth and inspects the bowl. He says, – I remember walking out to the wagon one day and thinking fuck me, I'm fifty fuckin nine. How the fuck did that happen?

Phil examines the side of Rawlings's face, ravaged red by weather and work. Tries to work out his age from the lines and creases worn deep with dirt.

– What you gonna do when you retire, Jeff?

– Who, me? I'm gunna sell me house and get one of them mobile homes. One of them big American bastards. Travel all round the country, stopping off at all different places. And I'm gunna get a fuckin twelve bore shotgun an'all, an' if any bastard tries to bother me I'll fuckin shoot the cunts.

Phil laughs.

– Oh, fuckin dead right, says Rawlings. – Both bastard barrels.

The older man checks the wing mirror and pulls the wagon over to the kerb.

– I'll drop you here, he says. – You have a good weekend now, and thank you very much.

– Same time Monday morning, says Phil.

Rawlings shakes his head. – Don't know about Monday yet. Job's tight. I'll gi'yer a ring.

– Aye, alright then, says Phil

He hops down from the cab and slams the door shut as the wagon moves off and into the traffic. He watches it roll to the top of the street and then disappear around the corner.

Phil looks up at the sun slipping behind a bank of low-lying clouds. From its position in the sky he reckons it to be about half past two, or thereabouts. Should still be in time to catch the end of *Jeremy Kyle*, if he gets a move on. He could do with a good laugh after work.

Eat Your Peas

Set of cunts, they are. I'm on those nets tomorrow night, end of. Had enough, mate. Lumping me up here with a load of fucking northern monkeys. Absolute fucking liberty. Cannot stick these Neanderthal cunts, me. See 'em all emerging on the landings every morning, scratching their arseholes and yawping their stupid bollocks. Like being transported back to the fucking Land That Time Forgot. Planet of the fucking Apes, innit. Well, I been a good boy long enough and it ain't got me nowhere so fuck 'em, mate. Fuck 'em right up their dirt box. Three requests to move ignored, letter to the governor in the box every week and not one word of reply, not a fucking dicky bird. The IMB came shuffling round a few days ago, some old Norris with a dodgy syrup and a crucifix round his neck, but they're about as much use as tits on a bull. So fuck 'em. I tried it their way, been through all the proper channels and they've took the piss, big style. Time for a bit of payback.

I know their game. Taking me outta my comfort zone. When they told me they were shipping me up here, the nut went into overdrive. No time to ask questions or lodge a complaint. Course not, just the old quick march to the gate and the long trek up the motorway to Coronation Street. Four hours in that sweatbox grinding my teeth.

Paranoia, mate. First thought: they're trying to set me up for a doing. Started thinking back to when I got lifted, all that bollocks they were asking me about out of town faces. There were a couple of northern firms floating about back then, as it happens. Mancs, I think, but fuck all to do with me, mate. I genuinely did not know who they were or what they were up to, never knew no names, pack drill, nothing. Those clueless Trident cunts though, they had me in every day for the first two weeks of remand, trying to spin together all kinds of fairy stories.

"Do you know Arthur-fucking-Buttercrumpet from Ecky Thump Hill? Have you ever met any of the Tetley Tea Folk Mob from Emmerdale Farm?"

Utter bollocks. It's London, innit, always different mobs floating in and out, but I never saw no dirty northern cavemen south of the river. Know a few different faces through friends of friends, casual acquaintances and the like, but they're mostly civilians. Sniff merchants and blaggers, yeah, but party heads, not geezers. Strictly social, mate. I never do anything with no one less they got the letters SE16 on their post code. Those Trident cunts, I just kept blanking 'em, and eventually they dropped it.

Then bang, two years later they ghost me out of Brixton and send me up here to the back of beyond. Fucking animals. They know as well as I do the simple laws of physics. A London boy up north? Gotta be a wrong 'un mate. People put two and two together and come up with five, 'specially these thick bastards. Questions will be asked. Seeds of doubt will be planted. Dirty monkey heads will be scratched.

They got the fucking timing right as well. Halfway through an eighter and my second shout for Cat D at the end of this year. Crucial period. They know full well I done all my sentence plan, completed all their Mickey Mouse courses, so they can't ask nothing more from me in that respect. All down to good behaviour now. First parole shout, no chance; yeah, alright, fair dos, but even the S.O. back down the road said I should be a shoo-in for my Cat D this time round. They're trying to set me up to fail here, these cunts. That was my first thought, that they were hoping I'd lose the nut and give one of these yokels a dig so they can keep me out of London on a weekend and lump a bit more onto my sentence. Trying to provoke me so I'll hand them my arse on a plate.

Dream fucking on you filthy animals.

First week up here I was on red alert. Anyone hovering at the door got a swift fuck off mate. No teabags, no sugar, no Rizla, get to fuck. Once the ground rules were established I slid down a gear, started thinking things through more rational. If they ain't got me up here for a doing, then what? What's the angle?

And then, one morning in the library, I saw the date in the corner of *The Sun* and it fucking dawned on me; her eighteenth. Sweet P. *That's* why they've shipped me up here, the cunts, to keep me away from my little gel on her birthday. I kid you not. That's just the type of sadistic fucking sick-minded stunt these scumbags pull. Evil bastards, mate. They know all the right buttons to press. Knew full well it was her eighteenth and now the bastards have made me miss it. Horrible sadistic fucking animals. Keeping a father away from his daughter on her special day. They fucking knew I had to be local for that. No way can she afford the dough for a train fare up here. And it ain't just the price of the ticket mate, it's the overnight stay as well. Hotel, train fare, taxis back and forth – it all adds up. Sweet P don't know nobody up here in fucking Emmerdale Farm land. This is how they operate, though, these Trident slags. Divide and conquer. Bang you away from friends and family, surrounded by strangers. Like throwing an egg in a pan and turning up the heat.

I done untold prison all over London and all points south, mate, and I usually clock a few familiar faces, people from all over the place, but I don't know no cunt in here. And that suits me fine and fucking dandy. Ain't looking to form no friendships. There are actually a few proper geezers knocking about as it happens; a firm of scouse scattered across a few wings and a serious looking Nottingham lot, but most of the others are all from fucking sheep-shagger land as far as I can make out. That horrible Yorkshire accent. *Eeh by gum, thee and thy our kid.* One man and his fucking dog. Never liked it up here, mate. Managed to avoid the place for the main part. We played Leeds and Sheffield back in the day and they both had proper firms and some of the clubs there were alright, but I never fancied none of those other shit-holes, Barnsley and Rochdale and all those other back-of-beyond manors. Some of the more childish element among our lot used to delight in terrorising the local farmer's barn dances on a wet Tuesday night, but not me. The magic of the cup? Nah, it ain't that fucking magic, mate. Newcastle, that was good though. The best night out up here by far. Proper. They were fucking stronging it up there, bruv. Two blinding nights we had down that dockland bit. Game cunts, them Geordies. Birds were on top as well, fuck me. Thought I heard one or two of the cunts rabbiting on in the library, but turns out they were Boro. They all sound the fucking same to me to be honest. *Why aye man, a fishy on a fucking dishy man*. I just tune 'em all out, as a rule. Load of gibbering fucking halfwits, mate.

It's burning my head out not seeing my Sweet P on her big day, though. I must have wrote about ten letters since I landed here, what, two months ago, but I ain't had no reply yet. Nothing, not even a post card. I shoot down the office every morning but my name ain't ever on the board. That ain't right - that ain't my Sweet Pea. She used to write every fortnight, regular as. Wouldn't surprise me if they were keeping my mail back, these dirty northern cunts. Probably wanking over her photo in the office on evening bang up. Would not surprise me one little bit, the dirty northern nonce cunts.

Well, I ain't fucking having it, mate. I ain't having it in the slightest.

Proper shit-hole this prison as well. There's bleeding ducks waddling about the gaff. Seagulls as well; dirty big squads of 'em sometimes, wheeling down onto the yard in a morning, screaming their nuts off and fighting over bits of waste grub, ripping apart them plastic bags full of leftover dinners heaped up outside the kitchens. They should get a fucking air rifle and pot some of them dirty squawking bastards out the sky. Fucking vermin, mate. Stinks of cow shit as well some days on that yard. Farmer Palmer spraying his fucking turnips. And I dunno how close we are to the sea but sometimes on a night I reckon I can catch a whiff of salt when I stick me snout out the window. Think I heard someone say there's a river near here somewhere, but that shouldn't be salt should it? Should be fresh water. Or as fresh as water can get after it's been contaminated with abandoned fucking prams and burnt out chip pans and shopping trolleys full of cut-price Netto baked beans and Yorkshire fucking pudding or whatever the fuck it is these cunts eat up here.

There's fuck all here in terms of facilities either. One basic education block with half a dozen steam-driven computers from the eighteenth fucking century, a poxy arts and crafts room with a potter's wheel and a scabby gym with half a dozen clapped out bits of kit. A library with a piss-poor selection of books, not even a fucking DVD club, mate. And of course the obligatory chapel full of grasses and nonces and bead rattlers, complete with an upstairs diversity bit for the Muzzers and the Buddhists. And that's about your lot, mate. There's fuck all here for me in this gaff.

Usually, I like to get out of my pad, keep myself busy, but there's fuck all jobs since they closed the woodsheds and plumbing shop so there's about fifty fucking percent unemployment. It's alright for these northern dole scum monkeys, they're bred to be idle, but I'm from a proper city and I need stimulation. I like to keep myself occupied when I'm doing bird or I go potty, mate. Two months in and the useless cunts still ain't got me a job. I'm on the waiting list for the library and the gardens. Outside of that, there's not a lot on offer. You can either fight seagulls on waste management or push a mop about on the wing. Or sit in a shitty depressing classroom painted dole-office-blue and read Janet and fucking John books.

Most of these cunts ain't bothered with trying to better themselves, though. They just lay around all day picking fleas off each other. Running in and out of each other's pads on the ponce for pitiful bits and pieces. I keep the door closed and bang out scripts to send back home. Law of averages innit; one of them's bound to get through the net.

It did occur to me that maybe the Fat Cunt was keeping the letters from her, insult to injury type of thing... but no, no fucking way would she do that. She would not fucking dare. Never mind miles of distance and walls of concrete and bars, the repercussions would be far too great and well she fucking knows it, mate.

My Peaches, though. Sweet P. She's all I can think about lately. Eighteen-years-old, fuck me. I remember the first night I saw her. She stopped at the Fat Cunt's Mum's for the first week or so, but when she brought it back to the flat, fuck me mate, I was proper shitting myself, I ain't ashamed to admit it. Worse than any fucking graft, bruv. I never slept a wink that first night. I was up and down like a tart's G string, checking her out every five minutes. I couldn't believe something like that could come out of me and her. So tiny and perfect. Her little toes and eyelashes and fingernails. I was terrified she would stop breathing, kept dipping me nut in the cot to listen. Couldn't get back down on the pillow till I'd felt her breath on my cheek.

Those first six months, mate, Jesus... what a fucking ball ache that was. That's why I ain't ever had any more. Could not stand all that crying, mate. Ruthless. Non-stop. Jesus, it used to tear my fucking nerves to shreds. Fuck that. Anyway, I was out the house most nights, grafting. Most of that first year after she was born I was bang at it. Nobody can say I didn't graft my nuts off for that kid. They got the best of everything mate, believe: plasma screen TV with sound fucking surround and all the channel bollocks, brand new furniture, brand new dishwasher, washing machine, fridge freezer full to the brim. Every fucking bill paid on time. Stress-free life. They were the best times.

Easy-fucking-peasy, mate. And Peaches, I loved the bones of her. Nobody can say that I did not love that little gel.

I remember writing a poem for her on her first birthday. I wrote it straight off, all in one go, didn't even stop to think about it. Something about her changing my life. Or me changing my life because of her. And there was a flower involved somewhere, some reference to her being like a flower. Anyway, the upshot of it all was her coming into my life and making it all better. It was quiet a good poem, as it goes. I remember reading it and thinking, yeah, that's not half bad.

It's all bollocks, though. You say you're gonna change when you have a nipper, but do you fuck, mate.

So, yeah. That was when I started to get proper pissed off - after I clocked it was Sweet P's birthday. I needed to do something, mate. Needed a head change, coz I was going off my fucking nut. A poster went up for a creative writing course so I went and had a nosey. I wanted some ideas for a poem for her eighteenth. What a total fucking waste of time. Laughable. The Doris they got running the course is a proper fucking lemon; drippy old hippy bird with a geezer's haircut and a mouth full of plums. One of those anorexic cunts what lives off birdseeds and brown rice. Constantly gulping at a bottle of water. Write your life story in fifty words or less, she says. Yeah right. Think I'm some kind of donut, love? I ain't giving you chapter and verse in the guise of light entertainment. We all know where that kind of info goes; straight to head office. I went to three of those writing mornings then I sacked it off. It was all police interrogation tactics. Write your life story out in fifty words. Think of a time when you lost your temper. Imagine you're blind – what sort of things can you hear?

212

I had a pop at one of her poxy exercises: "Think of an occasion when you changed your mind about something." I wrote about that time when the Fat Cunt went out with that slag of a sister of hers. P would have been about what, one and a half? Two? Not long walking anyway. Whenever that is. Anyway, the Fat Cunt had had one of her usual weeping dramas, said she couldn't carry on no more, she was always tired and I was no help and she couldn't do it all on her own and she couldn't take the stress of me maybe going away again and all the fucking rest of it. So soppy bollocks here agreed to stay out the boozer, keep off the stone and not go away with Millwall, do my bit around the house, all that nonsense. Cheeky fucking bitch. If it weren't for the dough I was giving her that house would have ground to a fucking standstill. Anyway, she went on and fucking on, so silly cunt here agreed she could go out with her sister and her mates for a night round town, some bird's birthday, friend of a friend, one of them. So I stays in with a bag of weed and some beers and fills the kid full of Calpol and stick her in beddy-byes.

I'm trying to watch a film when she starts up, crying for her Mum. So I gets her out of her cot and she stops up with me watching DVDs for a bit, Finding fucking Nemo and all that caper. We watch the fishes and then I'm like, right, off to bed madam. But by now she's wide awake and she wants another DVD but it's getting late so I cart her back off to bed. She insists I go up and play with her but I'm like, no babe it ain't the time for playing now, beddy-bye-byes time. As I'm tucking her in she says one more story then bed so I'm like fuck me, yeah alright, one story and that's your fucking lot. Soft hearted cunt, me.

So she asks for this book, I DON"T LIKE PEAS or EAT YOUR PEAS or some such bollocks, something about a little girl who doesn't want to eat her dinner. I find the fucking thing and open it and start reading it to her. Well, fuck me, what a scream. This story is all about this stroppy little gel who will not eat her peas. Her mother is banging on at her but she just crosses her arms and says I DON'T LIKE PEAS. Then her old Doris starts offering her all sorts of shit to eat her greens up. She starts off with little bribes, like bowls of ice cream and princess dolls but the little gel ain't having it. No fucking peas for her bruv, oh no. I DON'T LIKE PEAS, she says, sticking to her fucking guns. So the bribes get all the more elaborate and outrageous; a castle made outta diamonds, a supersonic jet plane, a monkey on roller skates; endless lists of all this impossible tackle. But the little gel still ain't having it and the list is getting longer and I have to keep rattling it all off and Sweet P, whenever it gets to the bit where the gel in the book says I DON'T LIKE PEAS, she joins in, shouts along like it's the funniest fucking thing she's ever heard in her life. We're both helpless with laughter at this stupid fucking book, mate. And the at the end, after being promised a spaceship and a paradise island and ten million quid and a speedboat with Beyoncé, the little girl agrees to eat her peas, but only if the Mum eats her sprouts. Then there's a close up the mum with her bottom lip wobbling and she says: BUT I DON'T LIKE SPROUTS! Made us both howl, that did. Then on the next page the mum and daughter were both having ice cream coz they both liked pudding. Blinding! Proper result! Anyway, P went to sleep after that and I went downstairs and fell asleep on the couch. And after that, whenever P was eating her dinner, I used to say to her, – EAT YOUR PEAS!

That's how I gave her the name Sweet P. That was her name from then on.

So I wrote this soppy fucking story out and gave it to the hippy chick and she read it straight off and got all fucking Sheffield United, started clapping her hands together and hooting with delight. This is a wonderful piece of work, she says. Absolutely wonderful! But what had I changed my mind about? she asked me. Guess, I said. To be truthful, I'd forgotten about that part of it, the point of the exercise. I just wrote the fucking thing. To me, it didn't mean fuck all, no deep meaning or nothing. It was just a story. She wanted me to read it out in front of the rest of the class, but fuck that. Make a cunt of myself in front of these monkeys? No thank you, mate.

Anyway, this hippy chick got all excited and asked me if I wanted to do some more writing. This time the exercise was to write a story from the viewpoint of someone totally different to you. So I wrote a story about that time the Fat Cunt went slagging it off round town, third time in a fucking month, but I told it from her point of view, all the things I knew she had been fucking doing until half past fucking four in the morning; all the geezers feeling her arse and all the chisel she'd been whacking up her hooter when she should have been home looking after her kid whilst stupid bollocks here sat in the house with a four pack of Stella and a porno for company. And how when she got back home her fella showed her who wore the fucking trousers, gave her a good seeing to, sorted her slag head out good and proper, mate. Three times in a fucking month, yeah? Liberty.

So I handed that cunt in and then the next week the hippy chick was being all distant with me in front of the other lads, the other participants, my fucking core group of peers. She'd only just recently started working in a nick, you could tell a mile off. Out of her depth, mate. She was young, posh and nervous about being around geezers. Half of those other sad cunts had only turned up for the free coffee and to gawp at her tits. I said to her, I said what do you think about my story, miss? She weren't having it, kept avoiding the straight answer, so I fronted her up about it; asked her how come she ain't gonna pin my story up in the corridor on the wall with all the others then, eh? I thought it was a fucking great story. She went all red in the face and coughed and spluttered and finally said it was misogynistic. I had to put her straight. Well, if that's the fucking case, I said, the story satisfied the point of the exercise, coz I ain't a misogynist, darling. I don't hate women. Not all women anyway, only Fat Slag Cunts.

Anyway, I sacked the creative writing bollocks off and went down the library and got a few books, see if there were any decent lines I could use. It was all pony though, either that Charles Dickens thee and thou shit or stuff that don't even fucking rhyme and you can't make head nor tail of what it's supposed to be about. I got a few books out, but there was nothing there worth lifting. I just used the pages for fucking roaches, mate.

See, what I didn't tell Miss Creative Writing Soppy Drawers was that I saw that fucking book in the library when I was looking for the poetry. In the kids' books section for the Story Book Dads thing – I DON'T LIKE PEAS. Saw the cover with the little gel with the knife and fork and the plate of peas and that's when I started proper fucking simmering.

Tomorrow night though mate, that's when I make my move. Have a bit of dinner and hang fire till just before bang up. Then smash the pad up and boot the fucking telly about the landing, put a bit of a show on. Soon as these thick-necked monkey screws come mob-handed, I'll be greased up and tooled up and larging it on the nets. Give these cunts a proper fucking taste, Bushwhacker style. Then it'll be a nice bit of seg, away from these northern cunts, read a few books, put me feet up for a bit, and hopefully get a ship out somewhere a bit more fucking civilized. Somewhere a bit closer to home. Knowing these snidey cunts though, they'll probably send me up to fucking sweaty-sock land. No problem mate, I'll kick the fuck off there as well, and every other dirty shit-hole they slam me in till I get back home to see my little gel.

Fucking liberty this is, telling ya. All wrong, mate. If there's one thing I've learned, it's kids need their fathers.

Christmas Is Magic

Police car crawling down the back ten-foot. The bathroom window is open a few inches at the bottom where I'm knelt, blowing smoke out. I can see the slow turning lights, the top of next-door's fence fringed blue. I shut the window and draw the blind. I lob the smoke down the pan, stand up slowly, flush the bog and drop the lid.

Me stomach's doing backflips and me first thought is, Oh fuck, the shed. But no. Can't be. I only put it there night before last. Unseen by human eyes. Made double sure of that. It was half-three in the morning, all the back-way windows curtained-off and black, everyone dreaming of Christmas. I wash and dry me hands slowly, methodically, bracing meself for the ding-dong of the doorbell. Calm, calm, calm. You have nothing to hide. You're a responsible citizen, going about your business in the comfort of your own home. Just act natural. Adopt the appropriate mind-set. How would someone who had nothing to hide greet the police on their doorstep? Surprise, with an overtone of concern. Yes, officer? What is it? What can I do for you? I practice me surprised-yet-mildly-concerned face in the mirror.

What if they want to look in the shed, though? Ask to see their search warrant. But that's as good as an admission of guilt, innit. Show me your warrant! Fuck me, it's not America. Do they actually need one? Aren't they supposed to be invited inside, like bailiffs? Mind you, if Angie gets to the door before me, she'll just let 'em straight in anyway. She won't even think twice about it.

Being half-battered is not helping. I try and calm me thoughts down and hope me heart-rate follows. Jesus, it stinks of weed in here. I'm supposed to go outside to smoke. Can't open the window again, in case the coppers are still there. Don't wanna attract their attention. Bastards. I get the Febreze out the cabinet and spray the room in a fine descending mist of antiseptic flowers.

Then I remember the bins. I'd gone to bring them in last Tuesday morning, only to find ten melted puddles of plastic and blackened rubbish, still smoking. Bastard kids. They'd done the full row. I said to our lass, at first I thought it was the latest council funded art installation. City of Culture, innit. Charge people a tenner to come and have a look. But it's no fucking joke, not really. Most of these back fences are wood and they could have all lit up like Christmas Day. Good job it's been pissing it down for three days solid. John next door has been out on vigilante patrol with a claw hammer every night since it happened. Reckons he knows exactly who it was; said he'd seen them hanging around the back way, smoking and fucking about, trying back gates and that. Druggies, he said. Said the floor was littered with dibs from joints. He showed one to me as we stood and looked at these burnt out bins. Held it up like Exhibit A. Joint, that, he said. I just nodded, grim-faced, like a side-kick American cop.

It was probably one of mine. I've been under orders to not smoke in the house since we had Jacob. If I want a blow, I'm supposed to nip out the back. I've been flicking dead dog-ends over the fence for weeks. I didn't tell John that, though. He's a complete fitness fanatic is John, all spray-on Day-Glo lycra and bulging biceps. Always off on fifty mile treks on his super-duper space-age racer, or pounding the streets like Rocky. Runs marathons and triathlons and all that lark. Scales mountains with weights hanging off his cock for charity. All that constant exertion don't seem to do anything to burn off his excess testosterone, though. He's one of them blokes who's always up on the balls of his feet, always scanning the horizon for summat to be offended about. Neighbourhood watch on steroids. Always someone parked in the wrong spot or blocking his access or some other trivial outrage. Loves a row, does John. And ever since Bingate, he's been even more het up than usual. Hence me smoking weed out the window this very evening. I don't want John springing out his back gate, sniffing the air like a demented bloodhound. Maybe that's why the dibble are here. Some poor unsuspecting young lad has wandered down the back way for a cheeky smoke and copped himself a claw hammer round the back of the napper.

No doorbell. No knock on the door.

I chance a peek from the bottom of the blind in time to see the blue lights recede, then nip through to the front bedroom window and survey the scenery through a crack in the curtains. I watch the car emerge from the Close and move off down the street. Yeah, off you pop, mate. Ta-ra, mind how yer go.

Me stomach's still doing gymnastics and I can feel me chest clenching. Flushed with the sweats an'all, I am. Light-headed, like I'm having a fuckin whitey, man. The rush off that J and the surge of raw adrenaline.

Calm, calm, calm.

I stand and watch the outside world for a few minutes. The tops of the parked cars and the roads seem to sparkle with the cold in the darkness. It's been wet, but if the temperature keeps falling rapid, them roads will be ice in morning. There's nobody about except a fella out walking his dog. I watch them pass under an orange street light opposite then disappear into the shadows further up the street.

Fuck this. I'm gonna have to clear that shed out pretty bastard quick, and in big chunks an'all - not daft dribs and drabs. I'm gonna have to do some leg-work. Take the product to the people. Last thing I need is a stream of visitors to the door. That would be the easiest way – everyone wants sorting out for Christmas – but our lass's radar would go off like a car alarm. Questions would be asked in the house. Not to mention Action Man next door, Day-Glo Johnny with his eagle eyes and ever simmering belligerence.

No, I'm gonna have to dig a couple of old contacts out, put a few calls in. Go places I've been trying to avoid. I don't wanna be fucking about like this, not really, but it's ten days to the big day and there's not a single present under that tree. Well, there is, there's summat for the bain from Angie's mother, but nowt else. I'm supposed to be sorting all Ella's stuff out. She wants all sorts. There's been a list stuck on the fridge under a Rudolf magnet for the last two weeks. A Frozen doll. Some books. A mobile phone – mobile bastard phone at eight-years-old. A fucking karaoke machine, for fuck's sake. There's other stuff as well. List as long as your arm. I'm supposed to have been on Amazon, sorting it all out. All in hand, love, I'd said. Don't you worry about a thing. You concentrate on the bain.

She's already started asking questions about non-existent deliveries.

I daren't tell our lass about losing the job. Make no bones about it, man, I'm fucking petrified. Not of her, like, obviously, but more the... confrontation. The anger. Obviously it's not my fucking fault, but that will cut little or no ice with her. The prospect of no Christmas, no presents for the bain, no nice food, no money going into next year... she's already half-crazed with lack of sleep and general anxiety. Be fucking *cruel* to burden her with that, wouldn't it? Next level stress, man. I will tell her, obviously, but after the event. After I've sorted everything out.

No, the last thing Angie needs to hear right now is that her partner has no bastard job. Wasn't my fault, though. My conscience is clear on that score. Colin had told me last Friday. I'd known summat was up for a good few weeks. Colin had been walking about with a face like a slapped arse. He pulled me into his office near knocking-off time and told me straight – we're losing money hand over fist, he said. We? I couldn't remember being a stake-holder in the company.

I knew what it was, though – he was worried about Brexit. Every scrap of rubber in that depot came from the Netherlands. Prices were already rocketing. I knew that just from skegging at the invoices and hearing him moaning on the phone every other day. Anyway, hard decisions to be made. Belts to tighten. Uncertain future looming, no guarantees. All that chat. He'd looked at it from all angles, he said, but he simply could no longer operate, going forward, on current staffing levels.

He tells me all this in his glass-walled office with his groovy little white Christmas tree winking on and off in the corner. I remember him coming in the day of the vote, all chuffed with hissen coz he'd got up special early to go and put his cross in the Leave box. Taking back control. That is actually what he'd said. And then I'm sat there in his office, listening to him bang on about his anxiety and fears and how he feels so bad about this, especially at this time of year, and if things look up next year, etc etc. That Christmas tree winking on and off. Fucking snowflakes and little blue reindeers dancing around. It took all my powers of self-control not to stand up and volley the fucking thing across the desk. But I kept the head and sat and nodded and said, yeah Col, totally understand, Col, and I shook his limp, wet fish of a hand. Merry Christmas, Colin, you useless cunt.

It was a case of last in, first out, so that was me and this other kid called Boris sat in Wetherspoons at half five on a Friday afternoon, nursing a pint of cheap fizz and wondering what the fuck next. Boris said he was gonna see if there was owt going in the Leeds depot, but fuck that, there and back to Leeds every day? Alright if you've got a car, but fuck me, on these wages, you'd be spunking half of it on train fare every month. I had no car, no savings and a four month old bain in the house. I needed summat a bit quicker than a vague hope of Leeds.

So the first thing I did the very next day was go and see Mr Brown. Well, no, that was the second thing I did. First thing I did was go and check the bank account and weep uncontrollably. But there was no time to wallow in self-pity. The chances of getting fixed up with another job this close to Christmas was next to nowt. My only option for short term gain was the Brown man.

It was a risky move for all manner of reasons. The last time I'd had owt to do with Brown did not end well and we'd parted on uneasy terms. I was never really cut out to be a drug dealer. Too soft-hearted for one thing. Too generous. And too fond of a party. It was the classic fatal combination. I'd lay on quarters and half ounces and ounces left right and centre and then forget who owed me what. A constant round of flats and back kitchens and fuzzy afternoons turning into comatose nights. Anyway, because I didn't write owt down (rule *numero uno*) it was far too easy for the less scrupulous members of my social circle to take the royal piss. I was also completely undisciplined with the money, failing to keep the pots of outlay and profit on separate shelves, so to speak. The end result was that every pound that entered my pocket flew out again hours, minutes, even seconds later. I lived like a King on a zero-hours contract.

When the cupboards were bare and it was time to settle up, I was a fair few quid short of the original asking price. Spending money has always been one of my greatest talents. Saving and earning it were a different story. Fucking Mr Brown. The bastard. I had to swerve the man for a month or so until word got back that I was on his wanted list, and I ended up having to borrow seven hundred bar off our Alec, who moaned and groaned and banged on about it for all eternity, but at least he was family and wasn't going to have me put in Infirmary.

Mind you, this was all a couple of year ago now, so I reckoned the B man would let bygones be bygones. I'd known him for time. I'd bumped into him on a few occasions out and about and he was fine, no static whatsoever, so I reckoned it was slate wiped clean. I was right. I could tell by his manner when I went round and floated the idea that he hadn't forgot the last inconvenience, but, being a fat lazy greedy bastard, he was more than happy to forgive if it meant me doing his donkey work for him. It was handy that I was in West Hull an'all, I suppose. I don't think he had anybody else over this side selling his grows. Not that it mattered. If you're not daft about it, knocking weed out is a largely stress-free low-risk activity compared to the other nasty shit. You don't have to deal with the desperate or the criminally minded. Well, you do, but it's usually the petty pest-like characters rather than the hard-core robbers and psychos. A nine bar or two can be weighed and dispersed with little fuss or volume over a short period of time at a workable profit level. Strictly friends and family, no door-knockers at all hours and no mates of mates, unannounced strangers. Easy.

Easy if you're sensible about it, of course. If you don't use it as an excuse to dip out of the nine-to-five and have a non-stop party.

Kids, though. I swore blind we wouldn't have another, but here we are. I wouldn't mind, but we'd sort of stopped having sex over the last three or four years. Any physical union between me and her was fleeting at best. I think she just got sick of shagging me, to be honest. I couldn't blame her, really. Can't be much fun going to bed with someone who's permanently stoned and pissed out of their heads. It was only after I cleaned up that she'd come near me again.

I'd only agreed to give it up after Angie threatened to leave me. Well, she didn't threaten, she actually did leave me. Took Ella an'all - went to her mother's, packed a suitcase, the full bit. I'm ashamed to say I didn't actually realise until about the Monday night. I was off out all weekend, buzzing about, doing me rounds, getting tanked up and twatted at various people's houses. Oblivious.

When I realised what the score was, I was devastated. Properly. I knew I'd fucked it and I was prepared to crawl over broken glass for forgiveness, but she wouldn't even answer my calls for a week. All necessary logistics had to be channelled through her mother. When I did get to speak to her, it took me another week to persuade her to come back. Had to promise the sun, the stars and the moon on a stick. One of the terms and conditions was getting a proper job.

So I did. I got meself in at A1 through our Valda's mate, Joanne. She was Colin's sister-in-law. I started off covering the odd afternoon, got a zero-hours contract and started proper. Built it up to more regular hours and a semi-liveable wage. Before long, I was Mr Straight-Head Civilian.

I also had to promise to knock the drinking on the head during the week. I wouldn't mind, but I hardly ever drink during the week. Just a few cans if there's a match on the telly and maybe the odd bottle of wine with food. Angie had stopped before Ella was born and never really started again. She'd have the odd one when people came round, but that was about it. Will power. It's one of the things I will say about Ange – she can resist anything. Including me. Especially me, if I'm honest. One of the many reasons I love that woman and would do anything to keep her. My Nana always said I could charm the birds from the trees, but my patter never washed with Ange. Read me like a comic, she could. If she was coming back and staying, she wanted visible effort.

So I stopped the bevvy Monday to Fridays and saved it for the weekend. Even calmed that down an'all, eventually. Mind you, having to get up at half-six every morning tends to slam the brakes on. Did me some good, actually, keeping proper hours and laying off the old River Ouse. I lost a bit of weight and started getting a bit of colour in me cheeks. Started to look and feel better. Nine-to-five, gym twice a week, five-a-side, proper clean diet.

And do you know what, I enjoyed it. It was nice, man. Nice to see the sun come up every day. Good to lark about with Ella before she went to bed. Help her with her homework. Times tables. The countries of the world. Read her stories at bedtime. It was good, man.

Proper good.

Me and Angie started to revive our relationship an'all. Her mam would have Ella and we'd go out, the pair of us together, maybe just on Newland for our tea, or a night in Queens, once a month or so. Testing the waters. I stuck to soft drinks, even on the weekends, sometimes. It was good. It brought us closer together. We went round garden centres on weekends, even though we didn't have a fucking garden. We even had the odd moment of passion.

That's when Jacob happened. Ella was made up. She couldn't wait to have a little brother. And then he made his appearance, kicking and screaming one night during the summer and there we were, the classic 2.4 line-up.

Yeah, we was living nice. For once in my life, I was properly contributing something other than worry and inconvenience. I was a lean, mean, fit and fighting machine with a conscience as clean as my freshly ironed work shirt. Had a drink once in a blue moon and a spliff out the back way on a weekend.

Family man. Loving it.

And then the chop, a fortnight before Christmas. A tiny mouth to feed and another one at school needing shoes and uniform and dinners and the loan repayment reminders fall like confetti and the rent man is knock-knock-knocking and it's fucking freezing cold and the gas and leccy are burning round the clock. And Christmas looming round the corner like that giant inflatable ho-ho-ho-ing Santa tethered outside the hot tub shop on Clive Sully Way.

So I got ten nine-bars off Mr Brown and banged it all in the shed on the Saturday night/Sunday morning, bin-bagged up and stink-proof. Problem was where to weigh it all out. I couldn't do it at home, no chance. Angie and the bain hardly ever left the house. So I had to go round to Sally's gaff and borrow her scales. That cost me a quarter straight away. I was there till the early hours of the morning weighing and bagging and smoking. Polished off a bottle of tequila an'all, between the pair of us. I had to tell Ange I was round at one of the lads playing cards. She would have gone spare if she knew I was round at Sally's. Apart from Sally being my ex, Ange can't stand her fucking guts. Says she's double shady and a two-faced bitch. She's right an'all. She tried to seduce me over the kitchen table when were busy sorting the bags out. I had to play along for a bit to keep her sweet. We had a bit of a lark about an' that, but we stopped short of the full deed. I saw it as a strategic act for the greater good. That was what I told myself anyway. I scrubbed me hands clean, filled me five-a-side bag with the weighed out bags and our reporter made his excuses and left. Crept home in the early hours and stashed the bag in the shed beneath a load of tarpaulin. Everyone asleep. Everyone dead to the world.

I stood there in the back yard and looked up at a sky bristling with stars. It was very cold and very clear and dead silent out there at half-three in the morning. I looked up at the moon and the constellations and realised I was an insignificant speck clinging to a rock revolving in a cold, dark yawning universe and in the grand scheme of everything it didn't matter if I fitted tyres or sold drugs or sucked off lepers for a living. I was everything and nothing and whatever shall be shall be. I had what you might call a moment of clarity. Our lass and the kids slept on, safe inside the house, none the wiser.

Such enlightenments are, however, always short lived. Reality has a nasty habit of kicking down the doors of the temple. And if having a hundred ounces of bagged up Harry Monk in the shed had made me a bit para, then them flashing blue lights round the back have made me double para with a flake and crushed nuts on top.

I realise I'm stood staring out the front bedroom like summat out the Hammer House of fucking Horror, zoned out, silent. The people opposite will think I'm some sort of voyeur.

Time to move. Time to get busy. I call Birdy and arrange to go round with two oz for him and two for their kid. Everyone panics at Christmas and gets double bubble. No idea why. Daft, really. It's only two days sat on your arse eating and watching the telly. Even the shops are open on Christmas Day, so I don't know why people feel the need to panic. They do though, especially bad stoners like Birdy, who gets a cold sweat on if he has to leave his house for more than two hours. And I'm only too happy to crank up the anxiety levels. Sort you out? Yeah, happy to, but you'll have to be quick. And I mean quick. Proper good weed this mate and I've only got meagre supplies, so fix up, look sharp. Don't get caught with your drawers down. Birdy says his other mate might be coming round and he'll probably want a couple of oz, maybe more. Let me know, I tell him, ASAP.

I put Tom Waits' *Step Right Up* on me phone as I pull a pair of socks out the drawer and hunt around for me trainers under the bed. Feels good to have a secret mission again, to be honest. To be doing something our lass knows nothing about. I don't look upon it as deception, though. In my eyes, I'm acting in the common good. What would she prefer we do, starve? No roasted bird on Christmas Day and no presents in the pillow case for them two beautiful bains?

Not on my watch, brother.

I find me trainers, slip 'em on, scoop me loose change off the dressing table and head out onto the landing. Angie's downstairs with Jacob, watching some bollocks on the telly. She'll think I'm going to five-a-side. I can just sneak into the shed, lift the merch and be there and back within the hour. I'll fire off a few more texts while I'm out, see if I can drum up some more business. Step right up, step right up...

I'm on the landing with me hand on the banister when I hear:

– Dad? *Dad?*

The bain, calling for me. Ella. I peek round the door of her room and she's sat up in bed. She's got that face on her. Eight-years-old going on twenty-eight. Swear I've never seen a kid who can look so serious. I tell her when she grows up, she's either gonna be a poker player or a judge.

– What's up, I say. – You should be asleep by now, missie!

– Dad, I wanna ask yer summat, she says.

– What?

– Can you come in please?

I go in and plant meself down on the edge of the bed. She's clutching her rabbit and her blankie up to her chest like it's protective armour. She looks so grave-faced, I have to stop meself smiling.

– What's the matter? I ask her.

– Dad, she says, – I'm gonna ask you a question and I want you to answer me truthfully.

– What?

– You've got to tell the truth.

– Have you been taking lessons off Mummy? I say, but she doesn't even crack her face.

– You've got to *promise*, she says.

– OK, I promise, I say. I hold up my hands to show no crossed fingers.

– Dad, she says, – is Father Christmas real?

Fuck's sake. I can do without this.

– Course he is, I say. – Now get yerself to sleep, coz d'yer know what, he can see yer, yer know! He can see if yer staying up late and not going to sleep like a good girl!

– How can he? she says.

– Magic! I says.

She just sits and looks at me and the expression on her face is so solemn that I almost burst out laughing. But she's not laughing. She's not even smiling. She's just looking at me.

– Hey, listen, I say to her, – how do you think he can make all them toys and deliver 'em all around the world in one night? And all on one sleigh, with just his reindeers and elves to help him? Gotta be magic, annit? I know it's exciting, but you gotta try and go to sleep, baby. And on the night, on Christmas Eve, right, the quicker you go to sleep the quicker he comes. And even if you try and stay up to catch a peek of him, you can't, it's useless. Resistance is futile. He just waits till you're conked out.

I give her a grin and ruffle her hair. She's got ace hair. Them mad curls. She's growing into a really bonny bain. And clever an'all. It's only natural she's started to ask questions. She's not daft. Top marks in her spelling at school. All her tests. Always got her nose in a book. Bright as a button, is Ella.

But there's something else happening here. The way she's looking at me, Jesus.

– Ella, I say.

– Please don't lie to me, Dad, she says. – Please just tell the truth.

– The truth about what? I say.

– Is Father Christmas real? she says.

The way she says 'real', it's like it's the end of something.

I don't know what to say. I just sit there looking at her duvet cover. White ducks on a pink background. Faded, washed to death, almost. Them daft ducks. She's had this since she was little. Always loved animals, Ella. I try and think of ducks, something funny to say about ducks, but I'm helpless. My mind is racing, full of everything and nothing. After a bit, I say, – He's real if you believe in him. If you really, really believe, he's...

– No, she says. – It's a yes or no answer, Dad. I don't want to know about believing or when you wish upon a star or any of that baby stuff, she says. – I'm eight now, Dad and I want to know the truth. Is Father Christmas real, yes or no?

Fucks sake. I'm not in right frame of mind to be dealing with this. Is Father Christmas real? I sincerely hope so. I could do with a visit from him meself.

– Have the kids at school been talking about it? I ask her.

– No, she says. – I googled it.

She looks away from me, like she's done something bad.

– I googled 'Is Father Christmas real?' and I found a website where grown-ups were talking about it.

And now I can see it welling up in her. Her eyes wobbling wet. Oh no, please, no.

I daren't say anything. I just look at her, helpless.

– They were talking about the best way to tell their children that Father Christmas wasn't real, she says.

The tears start to run down her face.

– You told me he was real, she says. – You said he was. I feel stupid now. I feel like a baby.

And that's it. She's crying now. Proper crying hard. Her body is shaking with it. She hides her face in her blankie and sobs her fucking heart out.

Oh Christ.

I gather her up in my arms and say oh Ella, oh baby, please don't cry, don't cry, and all she keeps saying is why did you lie, why did you lie?

I hold her while she howls, her head buried in my chest. I'm praying our lass won't hear it and come up the stairs to stick her oar in. Another thing I'd get the bastard blame for. I just hold her until the gaps between the sobs get longer and longer. Then she lifts her face up and looks at me. Oh God, her face. She looks devastated, the poor bairn. I feel a lurch of sickness.

– Why did you lie? she says.

– Listen, I say to her. – It was a... it was a nice lie. A lie for all the right reasons, I tell her.

– How do you mean for the right reasons? she says. – You're not supposed to tell lies.

She wipes her eyes on her 'jama top sleeve and doesn't say anything for a second or so. Then she says, – Who ate the mince pie? Who drunk the bottle of beer?

– Ella, I start staying.

– It was you wasn't it? I knew it was. You drunk it. It was all a lie. All of it.

She's wobbling again.

– Listen, I say, – this was different, this was a nice lie, coz... coz it made Christmas special and exciting and magical. If you believe in Father Christmas, it makes Christmas better.

This is precisely the wrong fucking thing to say, coz she bursts into a fresh bout of wailing.

– SO THAT MEANS CHRISTMAS ISN'T MAGIC ANY MORE!

– Oh, it will be, baby, I tell her, – it will be...

But she's having none of it, Christmas is spoilt forever now, it's spoilt forever. I'm pulling her tight into me, trying to shush her, but as sure as night follows fucking day, here come the thumping of feet on stairs and Angie appears in the doorway.

– What's going on? she says. – Ella, what's the matter?

Ella's pushing me away.

– Mam, she says.

– What's up, darling?

I stand up and make way for Ange to sit down and cuddle the bain. She's crying again, but not like before. Ange pulls her close, shush-shushes her.

She looks up at me. – I'll stay with her, she says. – You go downstairs. He's asleep, so don't go waking him up.

I can't get out that room quick enough, man.

I go downstairs and I'm pacing up and down in the kitchen. I look at me phone. Come on Birdy, you daft cunt. Does your mate want this weed or not? Fucking me about. I'm trying not to think about Father Christmas. I feel sick. I open the fridge for a beer, then remember we don't have any, that I don't drink on a Monday night, not even this close to Christmas, and I'm supposed to be still working in a tyre depot and not knocking out green or sneaking about in the dead of night or getting me cock out in other women's kitchens.

No, no, don't think of that. Think pure thoughts at the festive season, peace on earth and mercy mild, God and sinners reconciled. Which means you can lie and be forgiven. Which means...

Fucking Christmas.

The phone in me hand ding-dings. I stare at it for one stupid second, then snap back into the land of the living.

What was I supposed to be doing?

Fuck! The bain! I scoot through to the front room.

Jacob is silent in his carry cot. I kneel down quietly and look in. He's fast asleep on his back, the blankets gently rising and falling. I turn me face and lower me cheek down. I can feel the breath coming out of him, blowing gently against me face.

Peace. At ease.

I lift me face out of his cot and sit there, looking at him. He's still got hair, a fine coating of tiny dark curls. Like mine used to be. His tiny fists curled up besides his head. Hands in the air like he just don't care. Like he's surrendering. Small white heap of blankets and my son beneath them, his little heart beating, little pink lungs inflating, his freshly-formed brain dreaming. What's he dreaming about? Milk? Does he remember his dreams when he wakes up? I look at every inch of his face. Hard to believe that little face will grow older and talk and laugh and sit in pubs and raise glasses to those lips, kiss other faces, suck on the ends of pipes and butts, hover above people in the dark, do all the things faces do when they get older and learn to keep awake for longer. Staying up all night, staying up coz you're scared to fall asleep in case you miss something.

I should look at my phone.

I look at my phone. Birdy. He's heard off the other fella about the special offer and this kid wants to get on it. Another two Osbournes. Makes mental note. Type a response in the affirmative, in a bit. I'll get round to Birdy's and get started. Nine hundred quid. Ten more days. Presents, food, drink. It all needs paying for. And then more phone calls and more back kitchens, drinks, yeah, fuck it, why not. Christmas man, get on it.

I look down at Jacob.

I wanted it to be real for longer as well.

Angie comes back down the stairs and into the front room.

– She'll be alright, she says. – She's cried herself out.

– I didn't know what to say, I say.

– She'll be alright, she says.

She reaches down in Jacob's carry cot and touches the covers. He yawns and gapes, wriggles suddenly onto his side. For a second I think he's waking up, but then he settles and he's hard on. Deep sleep.

Angie looks at me.

– And you've been smoking weed up there, ant yer.

– No, I say.

– Yes, you have, she says, – don't bloody lie. You can smell it all over the landing.

She settles back into the recesses of her pillows and hot water bottles, flicks the sound back on the TV. I get up off me knees and sit on the couch. I figure to dash straight out would be an admission of guilt of some kind. I check the time on me phone. Quarter-past eight. I don't usually head off to five-a-side until half-past. I'm torn between wanting to get straight off and not drawing further heat down onto me already boiling head.

Calm, calm, calm.

I turn me attention to the screen. I'm watching it and I'm not watching it. Some bloke mixing things together in a bowl. He's baking something, slinging in the flour and eggs and whisking it all around. Now he's pouring himself a big glass of wine and he's banging on about how he used to spend his childhood Christmases in some little village somewhere. The picture cuts to him trekking through some snowy wooded glade and there's some seasonal orchestral shite playing as he wanders up to the window of this cabin and the camera goes through the window and rests on the glimmering light of this golden bauble hanging off a tree.

And now I'm thinking of that night when I was little, that night I was so excited and I crept downstairs to look at the Christmas tree. Everyone else was in bed, me Mam and Dad and our kid, me sister, everyone, and I plugged the lights in and just sat there for ages, staring up at these coloured lights twinkling and bouncing off all the ornaments and I must have been about, what, four, five, six? And they found me in the morning curled up beneath the tree asleep and I remember me Dad going mad about lights being left on, and now me eyes have gone all hot and there's tears running down. There's wet spilling down me cheeks. I'm trying to work out how I can wipe me face without Ange seeing that I'm wiping me face. I go for the casual yawn and eye-rub, but she's straight on to it.

– Are you crying? she says.

She sits up, peers closer, laughs out loud.

– Ha! You are! You're crying! Ha ha ha! You soppy twat!

She seems utterly delighted. After a bit, she stops laughing and looks at me.

– What you crying for?

– You know, the bain, I say. – Ella. Finding out like that.

I rub me face dry with the palms of me hands. Fuck's sake.

Ange settles back into her pillows.

– Yeah. Well, she had to find out some time. I'm amazed she hasn't said owt before, to be honest. All her mates seem to know.

– Yeah, but still.

– What?

– It's just... sad, innit. Father Christmas and that.

She looks at me again, her eyebrows raised.

– What? You're upset because Father fucking Christmas isn't real?

– No, I say, – I'm upset coz... well yeah, alright, I'm fucking upset because Father fucking Christmas isn't real. Alright?

– Awww! she goes. – Me bain!

Ange goes to put her arms around me, laughing. I pull away and stand up.

– Fuck off, I tell her. I start turning cushions over and rooting about, looking under the couch and chairs.

– Have you seen me shin pads? I say.

– No, I haven't, she says. She turns back to the telly, back to Christmas, still chuckling away to herself.

Ho-ho-fucking-ho.

I go upstairs and give me face a swill. Then I go to Ella's room. I open the door a nudge.

– Mam? she says.

– It's me, I say.

I go into the darkened room and leave the door open a bit to let a slice of light in. I kneel down beside her bed and stroke her face.

– Are you alright, baby? I ask her.

She nods her head up and down the pillow. She looks exhausted from all the upset and tears.

– Listen, Ella, I say. – Christmas can still be magic, you know?

– I know, she says. She smiles and reaches for my hand. I take hold of her fingers and they squeeze themselves around mine.

– It's alright, she says.

She yawns and her eyes close for a few seconds and I think she's bobbed off. Then she opens them again, looking suddenly puzzled.

– Should we tell Jacob about Father Christmas? she says. – When he's a little boy, I mean. When he's older?

– I don't know, I say. – What do you think?

She thinks for a bit.

– I'll tell him, she says, finally.

– OK, I say.

I'm not sure what she means, though. Tell him what?

I don't ask. I don't say anything. She's exhausted. Her eyes are drooping. She starts to say something, but is interrupted by a big gasping yawn, and the words fall away to a murmur.

– What? I say, leaning in. – What you say, baby?

– I'll be the grown-up, she says.

She's sleeping. I stay there, kneeling by her bed, until I can see she's properly out like a light, then I give her a kiss on the top of her head, gently take me hand out of hers, and I get off.

Freezing cold outside. I go out into the back yard and slip into the shed, pack the ting under me kit in the five-a-side bag. I sling the strap across me shoulder and then I'm wheeling me bike through the hallway, pulling the front door shut behind me with an almost silent click.

There's nobody about outside. No slow-turning blue lights or shadowy arsonists skulking down the ten-foot entrance. Even John's got his curtains drawn. Jesus, it's fucking bitter. I can see me breath hanging in the air. It's only eighteen ounces more, but the bag feels heavier than normal on me back. How many bags of green make a karaoke machine? I try and do the maths in me head but I can't think straight.

Birdy. Been ages since I seen him. Good laugh is the Bird Man. He'll have some beak in for Crimbo, no doubt.

I sit astride me bike and fumble about in me jacket, find a dib in one of the pockets. I fire it up and set off down the sparkling dark road.

If you enjoyed this title, follow Obliterati Press on Twitter and Facebook for details of forthcoming releases.

@ObliteratiPress

https://www.facebook.com/ObliteratiPress

Also, be sure to check out our website for regular short story contributions.

Also available from Obliterati Press:

LORD OF THE DEAD

Richard Rippon

A woman's body has been found on the moors of Northumberland, brutally murdered and dismembered. Northumbria police enlist the help of unconventional psychologist Jon Atherton, a decision complicated by his personal history with lead investigator Detective Sergeant Kate Prejean.

As Christmas approaches and pressure mounts on the force, Prejean and Atherton's personal lives begin to unravel as they find themselves the focus of media attention, and that of the killer known only as Son Of Geb.

Also available from Obliterati Press:

THE BAGGAGE CAROUSEL

David Olner

Dan Roberts has a troubled past, anger management issues and a backpack named after an abducted heiress. A chance encounter with Amber, a free-spirited Australian girl, seems to give his solitary, nomadic life a new sense of direction. But when she doesn't respond to his emails, the only direction he's heading is down...

'The Baggage Carousel' is a visceral yet humane travelogue of a novel about life's great let-downs; family, work and love. Dan Roberts is destined to go down as one of fiction's great solitary men, equal parts Iain Banks' Frank, Camus' Meursault and Seuss' The Grinch.